THE MIDNIGHT BEAST

Matt Hart

CORGI BOOKS

THE MIDNIGHT BEAST
A CORGI BOOK 978 0 552 55558 6

First published in Great Britain by Corgi Books,
an imprint of Random House Children's Books

Corgi edition published 2007

1 3 5 7 9 10 8 6 4 2

Set in 12/19pt La Gioconda by
Falcon Oast Graphic Art Ltd.

Corgi Books are published by Random House Children's Books,
61–63 Uxbridge Road, London W5 5SA

www.kidsatrandomhouse.co.uk

Addresses for companies within The Random House Group Limited
can be found at: www.randomhouse.co.uk/offices.htm

THE RANDOM HOUSE GROUP Limited Reg. No. 954009

A CIP catalogue record for this book is available from the British Library.

The Random House Group Limited makes every effort to ensure
that the papers used in its books are made from trees that have been
legally sourced from well-managed and credibly certified forests.
Our paper procurement policy can be found on:
www.randomhouse.co.uk/paper.htm

Mixed Sources

Product group from well-managed
forests and other controlled sources
www.fsc.org Cert no. TT-COC-2139
© 1996 Forest Stewardship Council

FSC

Printed in the UK by CPI Bookmarque, Croydon, CR0 4TD

TO BEN, KATE AND MOYA,
WITH LOVE

Chapter One:
Erasmus Slike

The satyr is perched atop a grey rock at the centre of a paddock fenced with white-painted wooden rails. His shoulders slump dejectedly, and his lowered head conceals his forlorn eyes. Every now and then he heaves a doleful sigh, and gives his tail a fitful twitch. His tiny horns are dull, the curly fleece on his legs is scurfy. A reed pipe lies neglected by his side. If the satyr wished, he could escape the paddock with a single bound, but if he did, he would not know where to go.

Once, he piped in dusky olive groves, and danced with dryads under a moon bright enough to cast shadows. That was in another world, at another and happier

time. Now the satyr is a prisoner upon the dull Earth, in the world of humankind.

Beyond the paddock stretch undulating meadows, dotted with copses of beech. On the crest of a nearby rise, glittering and glowing in the summer sunshine, stands a vast mansion of honey-coloured stone, with mullioned windows, ivy-clad walls, and chimneypots as twisted as sticks of barley sugar. This is Steyne House, which is situated some two miles west of the glories and grime of the world's greatest city, Wolveston. Steyne House is the ancestral seat of the earls of Bortle, and the current earl, Mordred Quincey Dexter-Coffin, is leaning against the paddock fence, contemplating the satyr with evident satisfaction. He is fortyish, plump, and has a florid complexion. His brassy hair is slicked back, his side whiskers are copious, his grey eyes are so pale as to be virtually colourless.

Not so his apparel: the earl wears an

apple-green suit, a lilac waistcoat and a cerise silk cravat, fixed in place by a pin whose head is mounted with a showy sapphire nestling in a cluster of diamonds. The earl's personal fortune may well be beyond calculation, but his dress-sense confirms the truth of the old maxim that the one thing money cannot buy is good taste.

The man who stands beside Lord Bortle provides something of a contrast, as he is taller, slimmer, older, and dressed in brown tweed. His hair is a silvery mane, his clean-shaven features are as craggy as a Highland ravine. There is a dourness about his eyes, and a hint of distaste in the set of his mouth. He is Erasmus Slike, a prominent member of the Parliament of the Commonwealth of Greater Britain, and he has just witnessed a miracle – multiple miracles, to be precise – for Lord Bortle has just given him a guided tour of his Fabulary Garden. Though forewarned

I
K
T
Z
G
A
X

of what he might expect to see, nothing could have prepared Erasmus Slike for the shock of actually seeing it, and the experience has left him stunned.

A mermaid has sung to him (her voice was rather out of tune perhaps, but still). A slumbering troll has impressed him with its ponderous torpor. He has gazed into the heart of a furnace, and discerned the outline of a glimmering salamander. Though he has not actually bearded a dragon in its den, he has hovered on the threshold of a dragon's den, and shivered at what lay coiled within. A parade of wonders has passed before him, wonders that he never knew existed. Precious few others possess this knowledge, for the Fabulary Garden is, almost, the best-kept secret in the land.

Lord Bortle is pleased by the effect that the tour has had on his guest. Politicians, in the earl's experience, are a tediously long-winded lot, and some are tedious before they have even opened their mouths, but Erasmus Slike has not spoken at all for several minutes.

Alas, this happy state of affairs is about to be spoiled, and Erasmus clears his throat before remarking, 'I must confess to you that I am staggered, my lord. How did you acquire such a unique menagerie?'

'Money,' replies the earl, with a careless wave of his hand. 'One hires explorers who go on expeditions to demon worlds. The pixie we saw earlier was netted in Fairyland.'

Erasmus baulks and blinks. 'Fairyland is a *demon* world?'

'My dear fellow, not all demons have talons and gubber-tushes!' chuckles Lord Bortle.

Mockery – bad! thinks Erasmus. Try another tack.

'Tell me, my lord,' he says, 'why did you establish the Fabulary Garden?'

Lord Bortle hooks his thumbs under

IKTZGAX

his green lapels, and puffs out his chest.

'Money!' he declares. 'When one is fabulously wealthy, one feels a certain obligation to invest a portion of that wealth in the investigation of phenomena which will be of benefit to the national interest.'

Erasmus is at a loss to see any connection between the interests of the nation and a troll, but lets the matter lie, as he senses his closeness to a point that he is eager to make.

'You must be gratified that your collection is so complete, my lord,' he says.

Lord Bortle drops his arms to his sides, and sulkily kicks a fence post.

'Oh, but it isn't complete!' he grumbles. 'Werewolves, you see. Can't get hold of one for love nor money. Tricky proposition, werewolves. Demonists who venture into their world tend not to come back – not in one piece, anyway.'

'And yet,' says Erasmus, 'legends claim that werewolves are able to visit our world. Your lordship must forgive my impertinence, but I have triumphed where you have failed, and I know where a werewolf might be found.'

Lord Bortle has been in similar situations before, and dispenses with any amount of dither and pussyfooting by baldly demanding, 'How much?'

Erasmus smiles. 'You mistake me, Lord Bortle. I require not your money, but your cooperation. Perhaps you have heard mention of the League of the Golden Unicorn?'

'A whisper or two,' confirms Lord Bortle. 'Some sort of secret society, isn't it?'

A fervent glint shows in Erasmus's eyes. 'A *deadly* secret society, whose members are fanatically devoted to the most noble cause of all.'

'What's that then?'

Erasmus drops his voice to a conspiratorial murmur. 'I'm not at liberty to say, my lord. Knowledge of such information may prove to be expensive.'

7

I
K
T
Z
G
A
X

'How expensive?' Lord Bortle asks roughly.

'Many have paid for it with their lives,' Erasmus tells him.

Lord Bortle wriggles his shoulders. He has the uneasy impression that he is about to become entangled in something far more complicated than he would like.

'What does this League of the Golden Unicorn have to do with one?' he says.

Erasmus is about to answer, but is interrupted by the satyr, who throws back his head and utters a loud and plaintive cry, filled with loneliness and longing. It is the most mournful and moving sound that Erasmus has ever heard, and tears spring up in his eyes.

'My lord,' he says hoarsely, 'are you entirely certain that these creatures of yours are happy?'

'Happy?' snorts Lord Bortle. 'They're not here to be happy, by thunder, they're here to impress!'

* * *

Upon his return to Wolveston some hours later, Erasmus Slike proceeds directly to Ireton Square, and passes through the marble portals of the Fairfax Club, an establishment so exclusive that not all of its members are deemed worthy of admission. Erasmus makes his way to the smoking salon, where he peruses the latest editions of the newspapers, while puffing on a Turkish water-pipe. All the Wolveston papers are available, with the exception of the *Evening Hermes*, a notoriously vulgar scandal sheet. To be sure, a copy of the *Hermes* is delivered daily to the Fairfax Club, but only so that the doorman can burn it in the street outside, in an act of ritual disapproval.

Since it is summer, and Parliament is not in session, there is little news worthy of the name, and Erasmus is relieved when his reading is interrupted by the

club's aged page-boy. Despite his advanced years, the page-boy can still squeeze into his tight blue uniform, and he still wears his pillbox hat at a raffish slant, though the lower portion of its chin-strap has disappeared into the folds of his neck.

In a voice as dry as the east wind in a thorn bush, the page-boy announces, 'Your guest has arrived in the dining room, sir.'

There are benighted corners of the globe where clubs forbid women to enter. Happily this is not the case in Greater Britain, which has long accorded women their rightful place in society. Erasmus has seldom felt gladder of this, for his guest, who is smiling at him from a cosy corner of the dining room, is the utterly bewitching Kitty Montez.

As he walks towards her, Erasmus permits his gaze to feast on her beauty. Her hair is chestnut, her eyes are blue, her nose is pert and pretty. She wears a red-and-white striped silk gown, and grey kid gloves, which Erasmus has never seen her without. Taken all in all, Kitty Montez is as lovely as a lily in a night sky. To glance at her is flirtation; to touch her hand is to be eternally smitten; to kiss her cheek is to submit oneself to a lifetime's slavish devotion.

As he takes his place at the table, Erasmus is careful to do none of these things, but he cannot avoid inhaling her sweet and exotic fragrance, with its underlying taint of unwholesomeness.

'How was your day with the earl?' enquires Kitty.

'Tolerable.'

'And what did you think of the Fabulary Garden?'

'Singular.'

Kitty pouts. 'Really, Mr Slike! I do believe you're teasing me.'

'That I am,' Erasmus owns with a soupy grin. 'You seem to bring out the playfulness in me. Odd, isn't it?'

'No,' says Kitty. 'How did the earl respond to our proposal?'

'Cautiously,' Erasmus says. 'He's pliable, but needs more working on. I believe that you might be more successful with him than I was.'

'That goes without saying!' retorts Kitty. 'But at the moment I'm far too occupied with obtaining the stone. Without it, the creature cannot be controlled.'

'As soon as you have it, I will cable Paris and let *a certain person know.*' Erasmus pauses, leans back in his chair, and regards Kitty quizzically. 'May I be direct, Miss Montez?'

'If I may be evasive in return,' Kitty replies.

'I am sworn to serve a sacred cause to which you, as far as I can make out, are not an adherent,' says Erasmus. 'I'm curious to know the reason why you became involved.'

'You mean, what's in it for me?' Kitty suggests.

'Quite so.'

Kitty's sparkling eyes take on a distant, dreamy look.

'The mayhem, Mr Slike!' she sighs. 'I simply *adore* mayhem!'

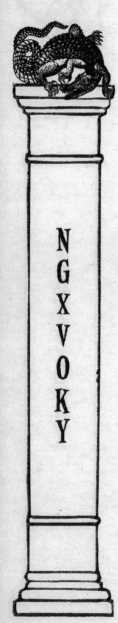

Chapter Two:
Thunder over Wolveston

A fortnight after Erasmus Slike and Kitty Montez dine together, and following a spell of disagreeably hot and humid weather, an evening storm breaks over Wolveston. Thunder rolls from one side of the sky to the other, and lightning cuts crooked capers. Rain falls in stair-rods and rapier blades, bounces up off the paving stones, and falls down again in a liquid echo.

In the smarter districts of the city, the downpour chortles through iron grilles and runs away into the sewers. In the shabbier districts, where the gutters are choked with refuse, streets are blocked as miniature lakes form. Nowhere are the lakes wider and deeper than in the area of Wolveston known as the Scarp.

The Scarp is as wild and lawless as any jungle. Every crime that human ingenuity can devise has been committed here. It is the basement of the Emporium of Human Misery: the guilty conscience of a great nation. Missionaries have vanished on its streets; reformers have been publicly pilloried, and pelted with a variety of filth. Its inhabitants are as close-mouthed as a miser's purse. They see little and hear less of what goes on around them. If questioned by the police, they plead an ignorance so profound that it is a wonder how they can walk and breathe simultaneously. Though human life is as precious in the Scarp as it is anywhere, death comes cheap. Hunger, poverty, disease and fear are entirely free of charge.

Here comes a denizen of the Scarp, scurrying down its main thoroughfare, Gospelmaker Road. He is a man, though

the light from such gas lamps as are functional reflects so glossily from his sodden overcoat and cap that he might be taken for an exceptionally tall and lumpy sea lion. The man's name is Waller Dolman. He is a night-watchman, and he is hurrying because he is already late for work.

In his youth, Waller took a fancy to a life of crime, but he has never been able to make a decent fist of it. On the one occasion that he attempted footpadding, his intended victim was penniless, and Waller ended up giving *him* money. During the course of a bungled burglary, Waller was apprehended by the householder, Detective Inspector Stott of the Wolveston Civic Constabulary, and was subsequently sentenced to serve eighteen months in Rollaway Prison. Here he sewed mailbags and dreamed of getting rich quick by becoming a forger, until it occurred to him that he could neither read nor write.

Though his present occupation is legal, Waller still rubs shoulders with those on the wrong side of the law, for his employer is none other than Wolveston's Mistress of Misdemeanours, Squalida MacHeath, the roots of whose criminal empire are, like the roots of a well-established bindweed, extensive and pernicious.

As Waller's boots splash and squelch through puddles, he conducts a muttered conversation with an invisible authority figure.

'Late – course I'm late, what d'you expect?' he wheezes. 'Have you seen the weather? There ain't no clemency in it. How's a man supposed to be on time when he's been drenched, draggled, and deafened by thunderclaps? How's a man supposed to keep body and soul together when—?'

Waller stops at the entrance to Scut Lane, a mean and crooked alley, and

cocks his head to one side. He hears a prolonged and urgent hiss, like the sound of steam escaping from a safety valve.

Intrigued, Waller steps into the mouth of the alley. No gas lamps shine here: the only illumination is the intermittent glare of lightning. Just such a glare comes now, and for the briefest of seconds Waller glimpses something sparkling at the far end of the alley, just as darkness returns and thunder crashes.

'What we got here, Waller me lad?' he says softly to himself. 'An oriental ornament?'

This is far from a fanciful notion, since people from every country in the world may be found in Wolveston, and the Chinese community has been here for as long as Waller has been alive.

Whatever the object might be, Waller is intent on examining it more closely, since he believes that he discerned a gold-like glister about it, and gold is irresistible.

He ventures deeper into the alley.

The hissing grows louder, and is accompanied by a slithering, sliding noise.

Orange light flares abruptly in Waller's face, and he shouts.

Fire roars.

Waller screams; then gurgles; then is silent.

A few hours later, in another and far more salubrious neighbourhood, the renowned magician Callisto plays to a packed house in Tuttleby and Hawker's Egyptian Hall. Callisto is tall, with black hair, green eyes and a sardonically wry smile. He is dressed in a black evening suit and a black bow tie. The stage he occupies is brightly lit, but bare: bare to its back wall, its emergency exit, and all the dangling ropes and pulleys that are used to fly scenery into position.

Outside, the thunder booms and the rain pours, but the audience pays no

heed, so entirely has Callisto captivated them.

The magician reaches inside his jacket and produces a pack of cards in a sealed carton. He removes the cards – and all at once, the carton has disappeared.

There is a slight ripple of applause; Callisto gestures to stifle it. He shuffles the cards one-handedly, grips them until they bow, then sends them flying up in an arc above his head before they come to rest, gracefully and neatly, in his other hand.

The audience sighs silently.

Callisto takes the cards in both hands and proceeds to shuffle them.

The audience disbelieves its eyes. Surely it cannot be – but yes! The cards are growing smaller. They are half the size they were when Callisto began, and now they are halved again, and now they are no bigger than fingernails; at last they are no longer visible. Callisto's hands keep moving, as if he is shuffling the atoms of the air to reveal what lies beneath. A small circle of darkness appears at the tips of his fingers. The circle increases to a hoop, a flywheel. Its circumference expands, swallowing the boards of the stage and a part of the proscenium arch. Callisto stands in an empty black spotlight, and still his hands work.

Behind him, in the dark beyond the atoms of the air, something moves. A teenaged girl steps out of the nothingness and stands at Callisto's side. Her skin is caramel-coloured, her dark eyes are shaped like almonds, her black hair has a blue sheen. Above a pair of baggy silk trousers, she wears a white shirt topped with a scarlet waistcoat. She is Aril, Callisto's exquisitely beautiful assistant and ward.

The black circle disgorges another figure: a lanky boy with a freckled face and curly brown hair. He wears blue

dungarees, hobnailed boots, and a red bandana has been loosely knotted around his neck. Under his right arm, he carries a bundle of kindling. He is Crispin Rattle, Callisto's other assistant.

A year ago, Crispin was twelve and had no family, no friends, no home and no prospects; now he is a star, of sorts. He drops the kindling, winks at the audience and delivers his increasingly popular catch-phrase: 'Watcher, mate, I've just come up from London – where d'you want your wood?'

This provokes a loud peal of delighted laughter, though several members of the audience find the remark puzzling, and others have to explain to them what and where London is.

This is the climax of Callisto's act, and the sound of the applause drowns out the thunder.

By the time Callisto, Aril and Crispin have removed their make-up and changed into their everyday clothes, the storm has abated. The air smells cool and refreshed as they leave the Egyptian Hall, via its back entrance in Paradise Lane, where a few members of the public lurk with autograph books. Once these have been signed, Callisto leads the way to Broadway Station, where they take a train on the Intrapolitan Line of the Wolveston Subterranean Railway. Five stops later they disembark at Bywater Station. From there, it is a short walk to their home in Scarlatti Mews, which they share with Callisto's melodramatic and indomitable housekeeper, Mrs Moncrief.

All day, Aril has sensed a seething restlessness about Callisto, and it has disturbed her. She wishes to put her mind at rest, and decides that now is the moment to do it.

'What's wrong?' she asks her guardian.

Callisto considers denying that anything is wrong, but denial would be futile;

Aril knows him all too well. He lifts his hands to indicate his surroundings and says, '*This* is wrong! This treadmill of working, going home, eating, sleeping, working – and so on. I'm stale. I'm bored. I want excitement and adventure.'

Crispin frowns.

'Didn't you have enough excitement and adventure when that sphinx thing whipped us off to the Land of the Dead?' he says.

'Yes, but it seems so long ago!' Callisto complains. 'I have to occupy myself with something.'

'You're not thinking of going after Bazimaal, are you?' asks Aril.

The look in Callisto's eyes hardens: this was the demon that destroyed his mother.

Chapter Three:
Mentions of Murder

In north Wolveston stands Execution Hill, where the last monarch of England was beheaded more than two centuries ago. No building has been allowed upon the hill, and consequently it is in an unspoiled state – part woodland, part gorsey heath. A popular spot for afternoon picnics and Sunday strolls, Execution Hill is also notorious as a location for nocturnal canoodling, and solitary females are ill-advised to repair there during the hours of darkness.

No one, it seems, has apprised Kitty Montez of this, for here she stands at the very summit of the hill. Loose strands of hair are whipped about her face by the

same wind that is shepherding the last storm clouds from the sky. She holds a curious object in her left hand. At first glance, it would appear to be a ball of amber about the size of a hen's egg; but amber is not veined with fat, neither does it quiver nor pulse with inner light.

Kitty brings the ball to her lips and murmurs soothingly to it.

'There now, rest. Rest and return.'

The light in the ball fades, its quivering stops; Kitty stows it away in her reticule, then frowns as the air directly in front of her begins to ripple. There is a sizzling sound, and then a demon pops out of nowhere, like a bubble bursting back into existence.

The demon is an ill-favoured specimen of its kind. Approximately human in form, its hands are equipped with fearsomely long black claws. The skin of its body is squamous and of a leaden colour, with a whitish bloom that resembles mould. Its head is shaped like a cow's, though it lacks horns, and there is a third eye in the centre of its forehead.

Most reasonable persons would react to such an apparition by fleeing from it, to an accompaniment of terrified screams, but Kitty Montez is evidently made of sterner stuff. She nods politely at the demon, says, 'Good evening,' and starts to turn away.

Few would recognize the sounds that emerge from the demon's slavering jaws as speech, but Kitty hears them as the word, 'Wait!'

'Wait?' she responds peevishly. 'Why should I wait? Do I know you?'

'No, but you know my master,' says the demon. 'He sent me to this jakes of a world to give you a message.'

Kitty pretends concern.

'Think of you, coming all that way just for me!' she coos. 'How was the journey?'

'Fiery!' snorts the demon.

S
K
X
S
G
O
J

'You must be parched. Can I get you something?'

The demon stamps its hooves, and gives off a smell like wet burnt-out fireworks.

'You're trying to distract me!' it bellows.

'True,' admits Kitty, 'and how tiresome it is that you don't care to be distracted. I suppose we had better get down to business. Who is your master?'

'Dargaz the Tongue-Stretcher,' the demon says.

'Ah, how is dear Dargaz?' enquires Kitty.

'Impatient,' the demon informs her. 'Dargaz wants the stone back, and if you don't hand it over straight away, I'm instructed to rip out your liver and lights and serve them up to Dargaz in a fricassee.'

Kitty laughs carelessly.

'How preposterous!' she exclaims. 'I can't possibly return the stone now, it would mean the ruination of my plans. I'm afraid you'll have to go back to

Dargaz and explain my position.'

'Explain?' the demon shrieks. 'You think Dargaz cares about what position you're in? Dargaz doesn't give a—'

Kitty waggles her fingers.

A swarm of maggot-like sparks cavorts over the demon from top to toe, and in an instant it is reduced to ashes.

Kitty regards the little pile of smouldering cinders with mild disdain.

'Good manners cost nothing!' she observes with a sniff and turns promptly on her heel.

At about the same time as the demonic conflagration on Execution Hill, the door of Callisto's house in Scarlatti Mews is flung open, and forth flies Mrs Moncrief, all knees and elbows. As a signal of her widowed status, Letitia Moncrief always dresses in black, which emphasizes both her height, and the boniness of her spindly frame. Her hair is grey and tied

S
K
X
S
G
O
J

back in a bun, and her nose is beaky. Frustrated in her youthful ambitions to become an actress, Mrs Moncrief has made a performance of her life, and she strikes a dramatic pose at the front garden gate, stretching out a warning hand to Callisto as he approaches.

'Mr Callisto!' she declaims, in the hollow tones of a hag foretelling doom and destruction. 'Miss MacHeath is within. I asked her to wait in her carriage, but she insisted on being admitted.'

'That's all right, Mrs M,' says Callisto. 'I know how persuasive Miss MacHeath can be.'

'Indeed she can,' Mrs Moncrief concurs. 'Particularly when she is brandishing a pistol.'

Hearteningly, no pistol is in evidence when Callisto enters the front parlour and finds Squalida MacHeath occupying his favourite armchair.

Squalida wears a grey silk gown with a

paisley scarf fastened around her shoulders. She is rounded to the point of voluptuousness. Her skin is creamy, her hair is dark, her eyes are as green as jade. She has an impish smile and a flirtatious manner.

'Mr Callisto!' she purrs, offering her hand for the magician to kiss. 'How delighted you must be to see me again. Where are Aril and Crispin?'

Callisto relinquishes Squalida's hand.

'At supper,' he tells her. 'I thought that we might talk more freely on our own.'

Squalida raises an eyebrow. 'Are you quite sure that you can trust yourself without a chaperone?'

'I shall be the soul of propriety,' Callisto assures her, as he seats himself on an ottoman.

'More's the pity!' sighs Squalida.

Her sigh causes Callisto to observe how tired Squalida seems. She lacks some of her usual vivacity, and there is a suggestion of dark circles beneath her eyes.

S
K
X
S
G
O
J

'May I make so bold as to enquire why you are here, Miss MacHeath?' Callisto says.

Squalida assumes an offended expression. 'Can't a grown woman visit an old acquaintance simply because the fancy takes her? Does she have to have a reason?'

'In your case, yes,' Callisto says frankly.

Squalida abandons all pretences.

'You're right, there is a reason,' she confesses. 'A most pressing reason. Over the past week, a series of ghastly murders has been committed in the Scarp. All the corpses were found partially burned, and mutilated in a manner that has made me seriously consider taking up vegetarianism.'

Callisto frowns. 'I don't recall reading about this in the newspapers.'

'What paper would bother to carry a report about murders in the Scarp?' Squalida remarks cynically. 'They would be more likely to celebrate the reduction in the numbers of the criminal classes than clamour for the murderer to be brought to justice.'

Callisto grunts, for this is a fair point.

'How many murders?' he says.

'Twenty,' comes the reply. 'The latest body was discovered earlier tonight. The victim was one of my night-watchmen, Waller. He popped his clogs in Scut Lane, poor beggar. I'll be straight with you, Mr Callisto, people in the Scarp are growing more scared by the hour, and it's beginning to cost me money.'

'How so?'

Squalida customarily exercises caution in any discussion of her financial affairs, and she is cautious now. 'One of my most lucrative enterprises is an insurance company, of which I am the sole director—'

'Do you mean a protection racket?' Callisto interrupts.

Squalida winces. 'That is not the term I prefer – words can be so ugly, can't they? Anyway, the long and short of it is,

S
K
X
S
G
O
J

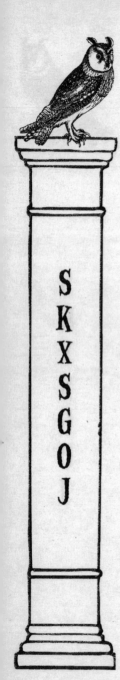

people won't pay up if I fail to protect them, and I'm failing. They're more afraid of this murderer than they are of me. I'm jealous of the fear I inspire, Mr Callisto, and I take a dim view of anyone who steals my thunder.'

'Have you contacted the police?'

Squalida's smile is sarcastic. 'A police investigation in the Scarp – hardly likely, is it? Besides, the police wouldn't be able to find out any more than I have. The killer comes and goes as he pleases – if it is a he. He leaves no evidence behind him, apart from dead bodies, and makes his way to and from the scenes of his crimes without being noticed. It's my opinion that this is the work of a deranged mind.'

'A very clever deranged mind,' Callisto adds in a murmur.

Squalida shifts uncomfortably in the armchair. She is not accustomed to asking anyone for help, especially a man. To her, a man is a pretty toy to be picked up, dallied with, and then abandoned when she catches sight of a prettier one.

'And I need a clever mind who will track the killer down,' she declares. 'Your mind, to be exact, Mr Callisto. Are you agreeable?'

Callisto feels a pang of excitement, for he intuits that this is the mystery that will deliver him from boredom.

'Completely!' he cries.

Squalida looks relieved.

'Naturally, I'll pay for all your expenses,' she says, 'but what fee will you charge?'

Callisto strokes his chin and thinks for a moment, before saying, 'My fee will be your company at a candlelit dinner for two at Vespasian's, after my services have been discharged.'

Squalida laughs huskily, as if the idea is not entirely repellent to her.

'Find the murderer, and I'll buy you the entire restaurant,' she vows.

S
K
X
S
G
O
J

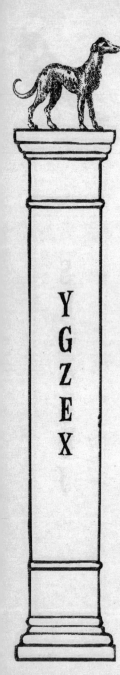

Chapter Four:
Extraordinary Meetings

Next morning, Callisto's behaviour at the breakfast table affords Aril and Crispin much amusement. They watch him in silence for a while, suppressing their giggles, then Aril says, 'You've got something on your mind.'

Callisto turns to her. 'And what brings you to that surmise?'

'The way that you're spreading marmalade over your kipper,' Aril says.

Callisto looks down, sees that it is true, and joins in the laughter at his aberration.

'I bet this has got something to do with Squalida MacHeath's visit last night,' opines Crispin, wiping tears of mirth from his eyes.

'You're both right,' Callisto tells his stage assistants. 'I meant to keep it a secret, but there's no keeping secrets from you two. Miss MacHeath has asked me to try and solve a mystery for her.'

'Prodigious!' says Crispin, clapping his hands together. 'What can Aril and I do?'

'Nothing,' Callisto replies gravely. 'The mystery involves the Scarp, a score of gruesome murders, and a killer who is almost certainly a homicidal maniac. The matter is far too dangerous for either of you to be involved.'

Crispin plucks the napkin from his lap, and casts it to the floor.

'Aw, swipe me!' he curses. 'Grown-ups have all the fun, don't they?'

Aril gives Callisto a disapproving look.

'You'd better watch your step with Squalida MacHeath,' she advises. 'I don't trust that woman. I'll never forgive her for having Crispin kidnapped last year.'

'But she behaved splendidly afterwards,'

Y G Z E X

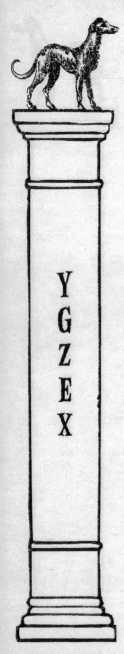

Callisto points out. 'I couldn't have come through my test in the Land of the Dead without her.'

Aril does not appear to be convinced, but further disagreement is avoided by the entry of Mrs Moncrief.

The housekeeper raises her right hand, in the manner of an Ancient Greek deity about to hurl a thunderbolt.

'Dr Antrobus has arrived to give Miss Aril and Master Crispin their lessons!' she announces.

Aril and Crispin roll their eyes, bolt down the last of their breakfasts, and depart.

Callisto ponders whether marmalade-flavoured kippers might be a sensational culinary discovery, but his curiosity does not extend to actually tasting his accidental creation.

Contrary to the morbid old joke, Necropolis Station is not 'the last stop' on the Extrapolitan Line; that distinction rightly belongs to the leafy suburb of Hazelrigg.

At nine-fifteen a.m., Callisto emerges from the concourse of Necropolis Station, and pauses to admire the breathtaking spectacle of the Wolveston Necropolis itself. Three titanic pyramids, dressed with Portland stone, tower into the sky above Cromwell Hill; a fourth is currently under construction. Each pyramid is honeycombed with tens of thousands of chambers which are intended to receive the remains of the city's dearly-departed. This solution to the tricky problem of Wolveston's overcrowded churchyards was the fruit of the genius of Sir Daniel Taffit, late-lamented engineer extraordinaire. In its impressive practicality, the necropolis is a finer memorial to Sir Daniel than the rather hastily executed statue which is to be found in Taffit Square.

The necropolis's main entrance lies at

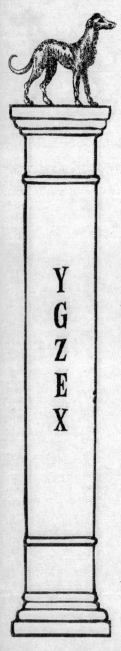

Y
G
Z
E
X

the end of Styx Avenue, which is lined with mature linden trees. The wrought iron gates are flanked by a pair of sphinxes, cast in bronze. The sight of these evokes memories in Callisto that cause him to smile crookedly.

The gates are kept by two uniformed guards who have been rigorously trained to keep out any unwelcome visitors – from vagrants searching for a place to sleep, to trespassers of a more supernatural persuasion. This latter group accounts for why the guards carry wooden stakes at their belts, and why their holstered revolvers are loaded with silver bullets.

Callisto is questioned thoroughly as to his business. He asks if the Chief Mortician, Mr Spaughm, would be kind enough to grant him an interview. The request is conveyed to Mr Spaughm via a speaking tube, and his response is in the affirmative. The gates swing back and Callisto passes through. He does not ask directions to Mr Spaughm's office, for he knows its location. Several of his past adventures had their beginnings there.

Mr Spaughm's office is cramped, and smells of formaldehyde. On his desk are a calendar, a blotter, and a brass-topped inkwell with a pen protruding from it. On the wall behind the desk hangs a large framed photograph of the unwrapped head of an Egyptian mummy, bearing the title *A Portrait of Mortality*.

Mr Spaughm is a large and melancholy man, lugubrious of speech and gesture. Below his bald pate, he has a face as round and grey as a dish of porridge. His eyes are rheumy, his lips are thick, his nose is minuscule. He offers Callisto a chair, then, with the deliberation of a loris, he reaches into a pocket of his jacket, extracts a snuffbox, and inhales two generous pinches of its contents.

'Always a pleasure to see you, Mr Callisto,' he says mournfully. 'To what

may I ascribe the honour of your visit – not, I sincerely trust, a recent bereavement?'

'Not at all, Mr Spaughm,' says Callisto. 'I was hoping you might be able to assist me in my investigation.'

Mr Spaughm closes the lid of his snuffbox, replaces it in his pocket, and withdraws a linen handkerchief. 'That, Mr Callisto, would entirely depend upon the precise nature of what you are investigating.'

'Murder,' says Callisto. 'Or rather, murders.'

Mr Spaughm sneezes moistly into the handkerchief, and wipes his nose.

'You are doubtless alluding to the activities of Slicing Tom. Have the police engaged your services again?' he enquires.

'Not this time,' Callisto informs him. 'I'm working for a private individual. Who is Slicing Tom?'

Mr Spaughm puts away his handkerchief. A rare smile breaks across his face, as slowly as a daisy opening its petals at daybreak.

'I see that you are unaware that the citizens of the Scarp have, with characteristic gallows humour, bestowed that nickname on the perpetrator of the recent atrocities that have been visited upon them,' he says. 'The sobriquet is, however, misapplied. In the dispatch of his unfortunate victims, the killer does not employ a slicing technique.'

'What technique does he employ?' asks Callisto.

'He tears!' Mr Spaughm asserts. 'He rends, bites and burns. He carries out his attacks with all the frenzy of a wild beast.'

Callisto's curiosity is roused. Past experience has taught him that what Mr Spaughm says is often less significant than what he does *not* say.

'Mr Spaughm,' Callisto probes gently, 'do you believe that Slicing Tom is, in fact, some kind of animal?'

Mr Spaughm brings together the finger-tips of both his hands. The office becomes so silent that Callisto can almost hear the dust twirling in the air. From far off comes the chiming of the clock in Parliament Park, followed by the tolling of its great bell, Long Tom.

At last, Mr Spaughm is moved to speak.

'I would not go so far as to say that I believed one thing or another, but some years ago I was called to attend to the cadaver of a circus performer who had been mauled by a tiger,' he confides. 'His injuries were not dissimilar to the injuries I have observed on the victims of Slicing Tom.'

The possibility of a tiger stalking the Scarp without drawing attention to itself strikes Callisto as remote.

'And how do you suppose that a tiger could contrive to inflict burns on the people it attacks?' he wonders aloud.

Mr Spaughm shakes his head.

'I suppose nothing, Mr Callisto,' he avers. 'I sift the facts, and base my conclusions on what I find. At the moment I have insufficient evidence to decide whether the assassin is a human or a beast, but I can tell you one thing about him.'

'Oh?'

'His confidence is growing,' Mr Spaughm says. 'At first, he hunted at the dead of night, and he preyed upon children and the elderly, as a pride of hunting lions will select the weak and sickly from a herd. Since then, he has progressed to the more able-bodied.'

'But only in the Scarp,' Callisto puzzles.

Mr Spaughm is affronted.

'My dear fellow!' he interjects. 'No decent district of Wolveston would tolerate such a thing. It simply wouldn't do!'

As Callisto's meeting with Mr Spaughm draws to its close, an extraordinary and clandestine meeting is underway in an

Y
G
Z
E
X

upper room of the Fairfax Club. Gathered around a long table that has been polished until it shines like a mirror is the uppermost echelon of the League of the Golden Unicorn. The meeting is presided over by Erasmus Slike, who has almost finished reading out a report to an intent audience which includes: a couple of vice-admirals, several members of Parliament, an archbishop, a newspaper editor, a police superintendent, the presidents of two banks, an arms manufacturer, and a bemused looking Lord Bortle. All are united in their wish to see a queen sitting on her throne again.

'And so, in conclusion, gentlemen,' Erasmus says, 'the first phase of Operation Osiris is underway, and proceeding as planned. Lord Bortle's creature is provoking exactly the level of panic that we anticipated. Superintendent Noakly?'

The superintendent is slight of build, and as highly strung and wiry as a terrier.

46

'The constabulary of our fair metropolis is dangerously under strength, underpaid, and its morale has sunk to the lowest ebb,' he says briskly. 'A major public disturbance would bring about its total collapse. The situation is excellent.'

Congratulatory murmurs circulate.

'Field Marshal Barkshaw?' says Erasmus.

The field marshal is the most senior officer in the Greater British Army. His face resembles a knuckle of pork that has somehow sprouted eyes and a white moustache. So many medals are pinned to the breast of his scarlet tunic that whenever he moves, he clinks like a pocketful of loose change.

'Staff behind me,' he declares. 'Loyal to a man. Champing at the bit. Trouble with this country, at peace too long. Need a war. Can't give Johnny Foreigner a kicking, Osiris next best thing. Thin out riff-raff. Toughen up national moral fibre.'

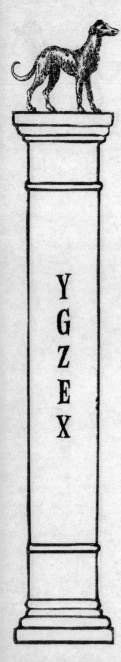

'I couldn't agree more!' gushes the archbishop. 'Armed conflict is so spiritually uplifting. There's nothing like the grim face of war for filling pews.'

Schooners are charged with brown sherry.

Erasmus Slike raises his glass.

'Gentlemen, a toast!' he cries. 'God save the Queen!'

Chapter Five:
A Child of the River

Night falls on Wolveston, and lamps are lit along the world's most renowned street, Broadway, the Avenue of Dreams. Among its myriad attractions are theatres – including the Egyptian Hall, where Callisto, Aril and Crispin have just begun their performance – grand hotels, casinos, restaurants both opulent and intimate, and museums of curiosities where, if so disposed, visitors may trace the history of dolls, or scrimshaw, or witchcraft.

One particular establishment on Broadway is in the throes of a remarkable boom in business. Like clothing and coiffure, eating habits are subject to the whims of fashion, and at the moment Welsh cuisine

C
K
X
X
K
C
U
R
L

is quite the thing. So it is that gourmets and the smart set throng to Cwm Rhondda.

Though small, the restaurant is not difficult to locate, as it advertises its presence by means of a six-metre-high papier-mâché leek, which stands above the portico of the entrance. The interior has been done out in rustic style: cart wheels and wooden pails hang from the walls; an ox yoke is suspended from the rafters. The waitresses are dressed in traditional Welsh costume, complete with lace caps, and tall black flat-topped hats made of felt. The waiters wear moleskin breeches, wide leather belts, and collarless shirts with open necks and rolled-up sleeves.

Seated in a cosy nook are Erasmus Slike and Kitty Montez. They have dined sumptuously on cockles and laverbread, followed by salt marsh lamb roasted with wild garlic, and served with a side dish of samphire. Dessert came in the form of the delicious Bread of Heaven, a variety of bread and butter pudding. Now Erasmus and Kitty are lingering over balloons of Mumbles brandy. During the course of the meal, they have put themselves on first-name terms.

The success of his morning meeting, the brandy, and the even more intoxicating company of Kitty Montez have conspired to loosen Erasmus's tongue.

'Where do I begin to thank you, Kitty?' he burbles. 'Before you joined the cause we were fumbling in the dark, but your guiding hand has—'

'Thank the stone, not me,' Kitty says dismissively. 'And I haven't joined the cause, remember? I don't care a jot about it. I'm following my own agenda.' She leans across the table and peers tenderly into Erasmus's eyes. 'You know, of course, that your cause is doomed.'

'Do I?' murmurs Erasmus.

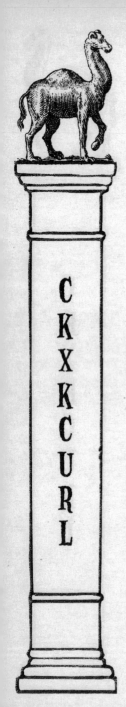

'The signs are plain to see, for those who know what to look for,' Kitty continues. 'I savour these moments. Expectations are at their most hopeful just before they are dashed, which makes the disillusionment all the more bitter.'

Erasmus raises his glass of brandy to his nose, and inhales its fragrant fumes.

'And why should my expectations be dashed?' he drawls.

'Because I have lied to you,' Kitty reveals in a low and earnest voice. 'Everything that I've told you has been a lie. You'll come to despair and death. Dogs will lick the marrow from your broken bones, and time will reduce you to a dust that the wind will scatter. Your memory will be eternally reviled.'

Erasmus looks ecstatic.

'Ah, Kitty!' he sighs. 'How thrilling it is to hear you talk that way. Is there any chance that—?'

'None whatsoever,' says Kitty.

A shadow is cast over the table.

Erasmus looks up, and sees Lord Bortle looking down.

The earl is incensed. His face is purple, his lips quiver as they attempt to vent his spleen.

'You, sir? Wining and dining with an attractive young filly?' he blusters. 'What d'you mean by it? Why aren't you fulfilling your end of our bargain? Why haven't you delivered what you promised? Why is it taking you so blasted long?'

Several diners turn their heads to gawp at the commotion.

Erasmus stands up, and fixes his mouth into a false smile.

'My lord, you're causing a scene,' he says through clenched teeth.

'A scene?' snorts Lord Bortle. 'One will cause a five-act play if one so chooses!'

In a tone of patient insistence that suggests his reserve of patience is close to exhaustion, Erasmus says, 'Your lordship

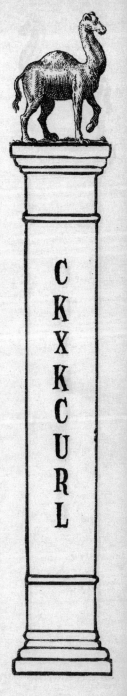

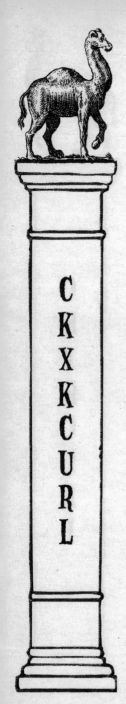

has apparently forgotten the need for absolute discretion that was explained to you in such painstaking detail. Members of our . . . club must avoid being seen together in public.'

The earl's face creases into incomprehension.

'Club – what club?' he mutters.

Erasmus's smile has begun to hurt the muscles in his cheeks.

'The club where we met this morning!' he rasps.

'The Fairfax Club?' says Lord Bortle. 'But one isn't a member of the—' A dim understanding – the only understanding of which he is capable – dawns in the earl's eyes. 'Oh, you mean the League of the—'

'Have a care, my lord!' Erasmus warns.

In a whisper that is not quiet enough for Erasmus, Lord Bortle demands, 'Where is my *werewolf*?'

The head waiter appears. An ex-miner,

he is a short but burly man with a broken nose.

'Everything all right like, skip?' he asks Erasmus.

'Perfectly,' Erasmus replies. 'This gentleman mistook me for someone else, and is about to leave.'

'Is one?' splutters Lord Bortle.

'Course you are, butty bach,' the waiter says, catching hold of the earl's elbow. 'You come with me, and I'll show you how the front door works.'

Erasmus waits until he is sure that Lord Bortle has left before resuming his seat.

Kitty smiles at him.

'You see?' she says. 'Doomed!'

Here is a thirteen-year-old girl, rowing a small boat along the north bank of the river Bast. Around her, the lights of Wolveston are spread out like a jewelled plain.

The girl's name is Dessica Flaunt. She

lives alone in a rented basement room in Proudwalker Street, at the heart of the Scarp. In her opinion, she is not likely to be living there much longer, as her landlord has taken to looking at her in a manner that she does not care for.

This is not altogether surprising, since Dessica is striking, if not conventionally pretty. Ginger hair, which she has, is unfashionable just now, as are large grey eyes, which she also has. Her nose tilts up at the end, her lips are on the thin side, but every now and then something beams out of her face with a warmth that would melt the innards of a steamroller.

Parents? Never knew 'em! Relatives? Ain't got none!

Dessica was not brought up so much as tamed by a retired schoolmistress, a spinster called Nelly Boot. Nelly kept her charge fed, clothed and disciplined. She taught her reading, writing, and the fundamentals of arithmetic. Then, when

Dessica was eleven, Nelly died, leaving just enough money in her will for the girl to purchase an old boat.

Since Nelly's death, Dessica has earned her living as a river girl, trawling the waters of the Bast in search of such items of value as chance might offer. It is a hard and uncertain existence, but Dessica is defiant, bold to brazenness, and somehow manages to survive. She is not alone in living off the river. At low tide, mudlarks venture into the thick ooze that lines the shores of the Bast to see what it contains. Dessica spurns mudlarking. She specializes in hunting for floaters: the drowned bodies of the suicides who regularly throw themselves off Wolveston's bridges. Dessica hauls them in, divests them of the worldly goods that they no longer need, and sends them on their way. Her continuing life may be the only good to come from their desperate deaths.

The river Bast is always eerie at night,

but tonight Dessica detects a tension in the air that she has not known before. She keeps her wits sharp, looks apprehensively about her, and witnesses a phenomenon. A bow-wave without a bow is advancing rapidly upstream. Just below it, something large is swimming with powerful surges. Dessica catches a brief flash of a red-gold colour that instantly reminds her of the tanks of goldfish in the pet shops down Gospelmaker Road.

'A goldfish!' she says to herself. 'The giant goldfish of Wolveston. That would be a yarn worth spinning!'

But before she can spin it, Dessica notices something pale bobbing in the ripples spreading out behind the bow wave, and she rows the boat towards it. It is a floater which, with surprising strength and dexterity, Dessica heaves aboard.

The body is that of a young man, and Dessica's expert eye tells her that it has not been in the water long, for the flesh has not rotted away from the face. She glances at the clothes.

Toff, she thinks. Namby-pamby. Drunk, I expect. Probably jumped in the drink after some flibbertigibbet turned him down, the great booby!

There are a few coins in the left-hand pocket of the jacket, and Dessica pops them into the leather bag at her waist. Fastened to one lapel, she finds a small regimental badge. Dessica knows nothing of regimental regalia, but she knows gold when she sees it, so the badge joins the coins in the bag.

As she explores the contents of an inside pocket, Dessica's fingers brush against an object that makes her heart skip a beat.

'A wallet!' she whispers. 'I've got his wallet!'

Disappointingly, this does not turn out to be the case. The object is a notebook, wrapped in a piece of waterproof canvas.

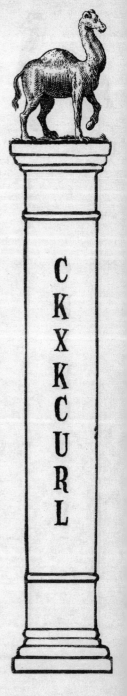

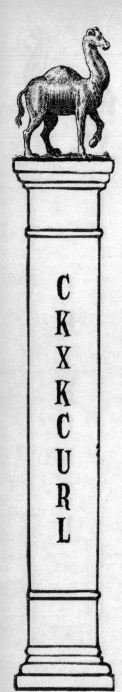

C
K
X
K
C
U
R
L

Dessica opens the book to the final page. The gas lamps of the north embankment provide just enough light for her to read the entry that is written there.

...and so the unholy thing goes on stirring up trouble in the Scarp by slaughtering more scum there every night. Before long, the situation will be out of hand.

But enough of this ~ enough of everything. I HAVE BETRAYED MY COUNTRY!!! I have been a blind fool. I obeyed FM's orders without question, and allowed myself to be taken in by the glib assurances of ES. At last the scales have fallen from my eyes. Tonight I see the League of the Golden Unicorn for what it truly is, a pack of traitorous curs who scheme out of self~interest. They care nothing for their native land, or its people. By following them, I have sullied everything that I once held dear. Loathsome as they are, yet I am more loathsome still. I cannot bear this shame. Only one recourse remains open to me, to die

by my own hand, like an officer.
The waters of the sacred river will
wash the stains from my soul, and
carry me into the Everlasting Light
that forgives all!

'Hmm!' comments Dessica. 'I was dead
right, he *was* a great booby.'

She speculates that the notebook in her
hand may prove more valuable than any
wallet.

'Well now, matey!' she says to it. 'I reckon
as how you and me should go pay a call
on Squalida MacHeath.'

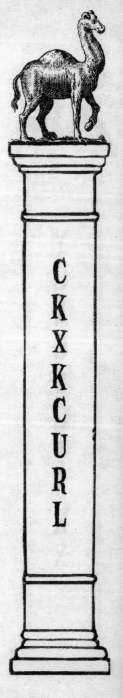

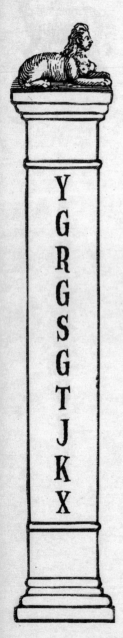

Chapter Six:
The Slightest of Problems

As she proceeds through the Scarp, Dessica Flaunt becomes increasingly conscious of the mounting fear that surrounds her. The Scarp is generally rowdy after dark, its streets resounding with drunken brawls and bawdiness. Now an oppressive quiet hangs everywhere, like a thick fog. Shadows seem gloomier, alleyways more daunting. All doors are shut, all windows have their blinds or curtains drawn.

And more than fear is fomenting. On dozens of street corners, groups of men stand smoking, and talking among themselves. Their eyes are uneasy, their voices are angry. The community that they are part of is under attack, but is unable to defend itself. People are being slain – and who cares in the outside world? The press is silent; the police do not dare to intervene; Parliament is on vacation, and even if it were not, would doubtless manifest its habitual indifference to Wolveston's poorest quarter. The people of the Scarp are weary of being neglected. It is time that something was done, time that action was taken – though who should do and act, none can say.

Dessica makes her way down Gospelmaker Road, and halts outside the deconsecrated cathedral of St Augustine's, a Gothic pile that is the hub of Squalida MacHeath's Wheel of Fortune. The arched entrance is decorated with gargoyles of a particular grotesqueness, and in front of the arch stand two dapper doormen, Mr Lipman and Mr Sparks.

A casual observer might well conclude that the doormen are twins, but a more

rigorous inspection would reveal that they are not. Both have fair hair, chiselled features and athletic frames. Both are impeccably groomed, and they are dressed in matching three-piece suits that fit them immaculately. The products of decent families and expensive private education, Mr Lipman and Mr Sparks met when they were young schoolmasters, and turned bad almost immediately. Their serpentine meanderings in the realms of criminality have brought them to their present employment, of which they are jealously proud.

Dessica mounts the stone stairs that lead up to the entrance, and comes face to face with its guardians.

'Stop!' brisks Mr Lipman. He looks this way and that at Dessica, and frowns.

'Here's a poser for you, Mr Sparks,' he says. 'Would you classify this young female as an urchin or a ragamuffin?'

'A pretty puzzle, Mr Lipman!' returns

Mr Sparks. 'Could she be something between the two? A ragachin, perhaps, or an urmuffin?'

Dessica scowls.

'Give over!' she snaps. 'I'm a river girl, that's what. Get out of me road, I want to see Squalida.'

'Not so fast, river girl!' says Mr Sparks, blocking Dessica's path. 'Firstly, sprogs like you should never refer to Miss MacHeath by her first name. Secondly, no one gets in to see her without an appointment.'

'An appointment?' Dessica gasps. 'I want to give her something, not have a tooth out.'

Mr Lipman opens his right hand.

'If you have something for Miss MacHeath, entrust it to us, and we'll ensure that she receives it,' he says.

Dessica takes a step back and narrows her eyes.

'I deal with the big boss, not the lack-eys!' she snarls.

'Oo-ooh!' hoots Mr Sparks. 'Aren't you the saucy one?'

'Ain't I though, dandy boy?' Dessica retorts.

'She has a tongue in her head, Mr Sparks,' Mr Lipman proposes confidentially.

'She does indeed, Mr Lipman,' concurs Mr Sparks. 'Although I must admit that I admire the cut of her jib.'

'There *is* a sort of engaging impudence about her,' Mr Lipman concedes. He addresses Dessica. 'We're inclined to help you, river girl, but we need more to work with. Can you give us some clue as to the nature of the article with which you intend to present Miss MacHeath?'

'A book,' says Dessica.

Mr Sparks inhales sharply.

'Oh dear, oh my!' he says. 'Not looking promising, is it, Mr Lipman?'

'The book's got stuff about the murders written in it,' adds Dessica.

Mr Lipman and Mr Sparks move smartly aside, and gesture towards the entrance.

'This way,' Mr Lipman says.

An hour later, Callisto is sitting alone in his front parlour. Aril and Crispin retired shortly after supper, and Mrs Moncrief was not long in following their example.

Callisto is grateful for the silence and solitude, as his day has been an exacting one. Subsequent to his conversation with Mr Spaughm, the magician visited the National Library in Threeble Street. There, amidst the crowded shelves of the Restricted Section, he pored over many musty tomes in an attempt to discover the true identity of Slicing Tom. His researches bore too much fruit, and he read accounts of any number of slashing, biting demons with a hankering for human flesh, with the result that a monstrous merry-go-round of Manticores, Catobelases and Chimeras revolves in his tired brain.

Examination of the victims' details, as furnished by Squalida MacHeath, have proved equally frustrating. If there is a link between the individuals concerned, Callisto cannot discern it. Either the connection is so subtle as to be beyond his wit, or the killer struck at random.

But only in the Scarp, thinks Callisto. Not in Broadway, or Highside, or Southwater. Does that mean something?

He is distracted by the clipping of horses' hooves, and the grind of wheels, then a knock comes at the front door. When Callisto goes to answer it, he is confronted by one of Squalida's liveried footmen.

The footman struggles with an insufficiently rehearsed speech. 'Miss MacHeath presents you with her compul— compil—' He breaks off with an exasperated curse, and says, 'Sent for you, ain't she?'

'Better come then, hadn't I?' responds Callisto.

He steps outside, locks the door behind him, and strides towards the waiting carriage.

Squalida MacHeath's office occupies the base of St Augustine's spire. Though modest in its proportions, the room is extravagantly furnished with Turkish rugs, old French tapestries and antique furniture. Sumptuously clad in an emerald-green silk dressing-gown, Squalida is recumbent upon a chaise longue. Off to her right, a ginger-haired girl who is more asleep than awake sits crumpled in a high-backed armchair.

'Ravishing though our reunion is, I intend to dispense with the formalities and get down to the matter at hand,' Squalida informs Callisto. She points at the girl. 'That is Dessica Flaunt, a river girl,' she says, then points at a small volume that lies on a nearby occasional table. 'That is the notebook she took off a floater that

she fished out of the Bast earlier tonight. It makes intriguing reading. I want you to examine it thoroughly and turn the intrigue into information.'

'I'll do what I can,' says Callisto. 'Was anything else found on the body?'

'This,' Squalida says, flicking the gold lapel-badge into the air.

Callisto catches it cleanly, registers the regimental crest, turns the badge over and espies a line of minute engraving. He snaps his fingers. A jeweller's glass materializes in his right hand. He holds the glass up to his eye and peruses the inscription.

'Captain Carlton Maroon,' he reads aloud. As he pockets the glass, a thought occurs to him. 'Forgive my asking, Miss MacHeath, but wouldn't it have been easier to send your footman with the notebook and badge? I fail to understand why it was necessary to have me brought here in person.'

Squalida's smile is radiant, winning, and entirely bogus.

'You've found me out again, you clever man!' she gurgles. 'I had you brought here because I have the slightest problem, which requires your assistance.' Squalida's smile is replaced by an expression of annoyance. She jerks a thumb over her shoulder to indicate Dessica. 'Little madam here refuses to return home.'

'I told you before, it ain't a home!' Dessica bursts out. 'It's a cellar in a doss-house, and I ain't never going back to it, and if you try and make me, I'll scram your face off!'

'You see my predicament?' sighs Squalida. 'Much as it would distress me to turn such a charming innocent out on the streets, I'm afraid I have no choice. I'm about to question a dock worker about a missing consignment of small arms. I anticipate a level of unpleasantness that would be quite unsuitable for a child's eyes and ears.'

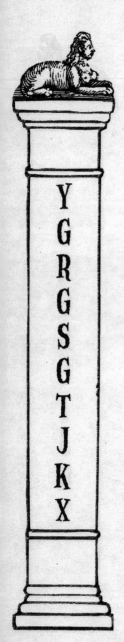

'Ain't a child!' Dessica growls.

Callisto knows that he is being put upon, and he knows why. Squalida MacHeath is far more soft-hearted than she likes to appear. She is genuinely concerned for Dessica's welfare, and by palming the girl off on Callisto, Squalida can be assured that she will be well taken care of, whilst preserving her reputation for ruthlessness.

Callisto turns to Dessica.

'Dessica – do you mind if I call you Dessica?' he asks.

Dessica shrugs. 'Why not, it's my name, isn't it?'

'If you would be agreeable, I could offer you temporary accommodation in my home,' Callisto offers.

Dessica regards him with suspicious hostility. 'Here! What's your game, Mr Smooth Talker?'

'Girl, do you trust me?' Squalida interrupts.

'A bit,' mumbles Dessica.

'Then trust me when I tell you that you can trust Mr Callisto!' Squalida asserts.

Dessica's mouth drops open.

'Callisto?' she squeaks. 'The feller off of the stage? The conjuror?'

'The very same,' confirms Callisto.

'Well I'll be hugged by hippos!' Dessica says with a giggle.

Shortly afterwards, a carriage containing Callisto and the slumbering Dessica Flaunt drives through Bearwood Street, on the outer fringes of the Scarp. Callisto has let down one of the carriage windows so that he can stare at the night sky. A full moon is due, and Callisto reflects that he and Crispin will have to manage their stage act without Aril for a day or so.

Dessica moans; her arms stir.

'Keep off!' she mutters. 'You come near

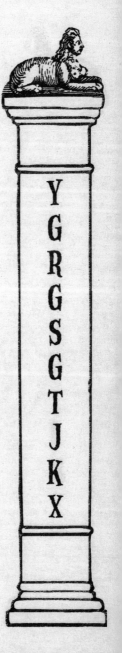

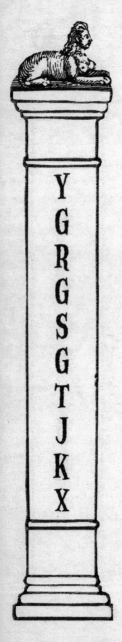

me again, you'll get my shiv in your guts!'

Callisto is uncertain whether she is speaking to him, or to something that haunts her dreams.

Chapter Seven:
The Appalling Intent

At Scarlatti Mews, Callisto installs Dessica in the front parlour, erects a camp bed, provides her with a face flannel and a towel, and informs her of the bathroom's whereabouts. Dessica drowsily half-listens, convinced that she is asleep, and that when she wakes in the morning she will find herself back in her Proudwalker Street crib.

Callisto pencils a note to Mrs Moncrief, forewarning her of the newcomer's presence. He leaves the note on the kitchen table before going upstairs to his room. Here he lights an oil lamp, removes his tie, loosens his collar and settles down to inspect the notebook. The peaceful

H
G
Y
O
R
O
Y
Q

isolation he experienced earlier returns. Callisto's mind sings as it embarks upon the kind of activity it most relishes: answering riddles, solving puzzles, fitting fragments together. The magician appreciates a complex problem as others might appreciate an exquisite item of jewellery.

He begins with the assumption that the man named on the regimental badge, Captain Carlton Maroon, and the owner of the notebook are one and the same. This is given added credence by a small sticker inside the front cover, which advertises the fact that the volume was supplied by Aitken and Chumm of Broadway, the most fashionable stationers' shop in Wolveston. It is highly probable that a smart officer would patronize such an establishment, preferring its stock to the shoddy offerings of Army Standard Issue.

The other truths buried in the notebook reveal themselves more circumspectly.

The entries are in code, except for

the final entry, whose frenzied scrawl offers considerable insight into Captain Maroon's emotional state. At the last, he was in too much of a rush to bother with encryption.

The last page reads:

SQ HBJED CQ HEED
SQ FJQYD VYHIJ MEBLUIJED
BQ DSU HI
JEEBXQC RQ HHQSAI

Now Callisto makes a second assumption. Since Greater Britain is neither at war nor under threat of war, military personnel are unlikely to be versed in the more rigorous branches of cryptography, and therefore the notebook's code is almost certainly relatively straightforward. Proceeding accordingly, Callisto starts with one of the simplest codes, Caesar's Cipher, which was reputedly the invention of the famous general and dictator, Julius Caesar. The cipher

operates by shifting the letters of the alphabet a certain number of places. A shift of one place would cause the letter *A* to be coded as *B*, *B* as *C* and so on until *Z*, which would be coded as A. Presuming that the groups of letters in the inscription represent English words, Callisto counts the number of times that each letter is used, and finds that Q is the clear leader. Since he knows that E is the most frequently written letter in English, he takes a sheet of squared paper, writes out the alphabet, then writes a second alphabet beneath it, starting with M, so that Q on the lower line coincides with E on the upper. Using this cipher, the first word of the inscription decodes as *GEVPXSR*.

Undeterred, Callisto writes out the alphabet again, and beneath writes an alphabet in which Q represents *T*, the second most-frequently written letter. Once more, the result is nonsense.

But on the third attempt, using an alphabet in which Q stands for the next most common letter, *A*, the inscription reads:

CARLTON MAROON

CAPTAIN FIRST WOLVESTON LANCERS

TOOLHAM BARRACKS

The key has turned, the door has yielded. Callisto begins to make a transcription of the decrypted entries. The lateness of the hour matters nothing to him. His fatigue vanishes in the all-consuming thrill of discovery.

The notebook covers a period of just over eighteen months in Captain Maroon's life, commencing with his posting to Toolham Barracks.

My quarters are tolerable. My fellow officers are rather stand-offish.

The catering is execrable —
tonight's offering consisted of
brown soup and boiled mutton
with dumplings.

For the first few weeks, Captain
Maroon gives the impression of being
excruciatingly bored.

I walked backwards around the
parade ground this morning.
Tomorrow, sideways.

Eventually the captain begins to make
friends.

DC and I went hunting mushrooms
in Toolham Woods. Shot five.
Spiffing fun.

Before long, and almost inevitably, the
captain is seduced by the delights of
nearby Wolveston, and the entries catalogue the capital's music halls, dancing
girls and casinos.

*Last night, dined at Cwm Rhondda
with F. We went on to Tawder's
Gaming Rooms, where I lost heavily.
What a cursed fool I am! Why do I
squander my money and time in
dens of iniquity, keeping company
with floozies, rogues and scoundrels?
Yet I must return to Tawder's
tonight.*

By Yuletide, the captain is experiencing considerable difficulty in honouring his gambling debts, and his thoughts take a decidedly gloomy turn.

*It is Christmas Day. Of all the
days in the year, this is the one
that ought to fill me with good
cheer ~ yet I am grey and
despondent. Father was right when
he said that I would turn out
to be a thoroughly bad lot. I can
stick to nothing except excess, and
I face ruin. Should I end my
miserable existence with my pistol?
Inconsiderate. Think of the mess
that would have to be cleared up
Throw myself under a train?*

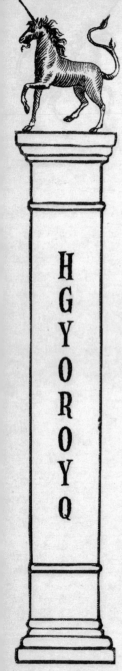

Selfish. It would disrupt timetables and discomfort innocent travellers. Drowning? Convenient and economic, but chilly. I shall reconsider when the weather is warmer.

Then, in spring, something intriguing occurs.

I had a long chin~wag with DC, regarding the state of the country. DC is a capital fellow who knows what's what. I wish I had his turn of phrase. We both agreed that the nation has gone to the dogs. The ruffian element is on the up and up. Every town is choked with beggars who are just too plain lazy to seek employment. The homeless revel in the squalor of the streets ~ or else why would they live there? Drunkenness and vice are rampant, and the younger generation is utterly spoilt and spineless. The Commonwealth is rotting from within, and democracy has failed the populace. It's time for a change, time to look back at former glories *instead of peering into an uncertain future. DC is quite right, voting changes nothing, and the people are weary of it. They want to be told what to do. The country needs to obey orders, not be presented with choices. If only the past could be set right!*

In the autumn, Captain Maroon's circumstances undergo a crisis, and a transformation.

Today I was hauled up before the CO. To my mortification, FM was present. The CO waved a bundle of my IOUs under my nose, and put a flea in my ear. He told me I was dissolute and weak ～ true, all true! ～ and that I was a disgrace to the regiment. If he had his way, I would be stripped to the waist and publicly flogged. Then the CO had a foaming fit and had to report himself to the MO, leaving me alone with FM. Avuncular sort. Riffled through the IOUs and tipped me a wink. Youthful high jinks, nothing

serious. DC told him I was the right
sort, which is the main thing. Big
smile. If I would agree to cooperate,
FM would ensure disappearance of
debts. Flabbergasted and banjaxed —
cooperate with what? FM explained.
MS IS THE ANSWER TO
EVERYTHING! She is the way
forwards into the sunlit uplands.
FM a genius. Man of few, but
brilliant, words. Upshot of conversation:
Scarp a festering boil, must be lanced
and drained. Instigate panic to
provoke violence and rioting
Constabulary unable to cope. Army
called in, martial law declared. Scarp
decimated, control regained. FM
dissolves Parliament, dismisses
Lord Protector; establishes military
junta. MS invited to take the
throne. New world. Poverty eradicated
by extermination of poor. National
character purged of foreign taints.
Pure blood. Idlers and undesirables
sent to Labour Centres and forced to
work for their food. Spread system
to other countries by making war
on them. War good for economy.
Eventually, whole world at war, every
country happy and prosperous.

I PLEDGE MY LIFE TO THE LEAGUE OF THE GOLDEN UNICORN!

From this point onwards, the captain devotes himself to his new-found cause, becomes a trusted confidant of FM, and is present at several of his secret meetings with ES, who is evidently a politician of some kind. The entries grow sketchy, hardly more than lists of dates and times; people and places are a jumble of initials, such as, *July 7th 2.30 to S with FM to meet SN. 4, AW.*

After a score or so pages of such stuff, Callisto happens upon a passage that causes him to sit bolt upright.

With FM and ES to SH to meet LB. Merciful Heaven, what a sink of infernal depravity! A place where legendary abominations move, breathe and have their being. I have looked into the eyes of the Scarp's Nemesis, and felt my courage melt.

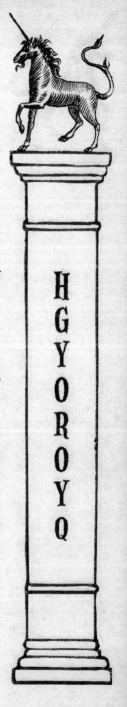

It is the terror of a nightmare made flesh. Can the will of such an unhallowed brute be bent to serve the Righteous Cause?
The cause of M.S.
Mariah Stuart.
Mariah R.
Mariah, Queen of England.

The random shards drop into a kaleidoscopic pattern, and Callisto gasps. The room seems to swirl around him, and for a moment it is as if all his solid certainties have turned to vapour. He knows whom Captain Maroon was pledged to serve, and he understands the appalling intent of the League of the Golden Unicorn.

Its fellowship is dedicated to the Restoration of the Monarchy. And the beast stalking the Scarp is somehow helping them. But how? And who is controlling it?

Chapter Eight:
In the Mists of Morning

At daybreak, a dense mist hangs over the river Bast and extends itself into the stirring city. It enswathes Parliament Park, where Erasmus Slike and Kitty Montez amble among the flower-beds and statuary. The Parliament Building is indistinct amid the misty whiteness, a blurry suggestion of towers and cupolas.

Erasmus and Kitty linger at the foot of the equestrian statue of General Cromwell, the country's first, if somewhat inept, Lord Protector. Cromwell is depicted in armour, ready for battle. His face is stern and warty. The tresses of his long bronze hair fall in a frozen tumble to his shoulders.

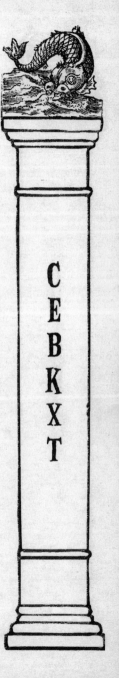

C
E
B
K
X
T

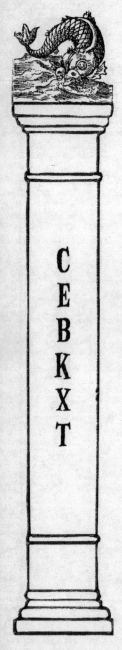

Erasmus has been awake all night, and is delirious with love for Kitty. The many feelings that he denied himself as a younger man now flood his middle age, and carry him along like plankton in an ocean current. He waves his hand to indicate Cromwell, and in a voice thick with wine and lack of sleep, asks, 'Are there many memorial statues in your part of the world, Kitty?'

'No, only statues that make people forget,' Kitty replies.

Erasmus looks at her curiously.

'Where is your part of the world, exactly?' he says.

'Abroad,' declares Kitty. 'Think far-off, and then some.'

'You speak excellent English.'

As fond of flattery as she is, Kitty Montez is nevertheless entirely immune to it.

'I can't speak a word of English,' she reveals, 'though I can make everyone think that I do.'

Erasmus regards Cromwell with a baleful eye.

'It's all his fault,' he says. 'If that country bumpkin hadn't won the war, and ordered the execution of the king, the country wouldn't be in the sorry state that it is today.'

'That's all my eye!' retorts Kitty. 'When the war ended, the same people were rich and poor as before it began. The wealthy still held banquets while the paupers starved. Justice was still available to those who could afford the wiliest lawyers. Politicians are a good deal less influential than they think themselves. They're good for generating paperwork, but it's rare for one of them to actually change anything.'

'Chancellor Dagwoody did!' Erasmus objects. 'He raised the import duty on foreign dolls with blue eyes, to encourage the Greater British toy industry.'

'Bully for him!' Kitty sneers. 'But that's enough talk of politics. Let's discuss me

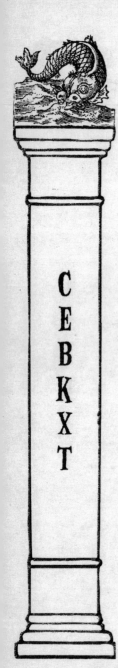

instead. Are you infatuated with me, or besotted?'

'I am enslaved!' Erasmus exclaims extravagantly.

Kitty tuts, and shakes her head.

'You're not enslaved yet,' she says. 'I know what it is to be a slave, and believe you me, it's far more disagreeable than anything I've put you through. What would you do to please me?'

'Anything!' Erasmus says, throwing his arms wide.

'Parade down Broadway, clad only in your combinations?' proposes Kitty.

'Without a thought.'

'Burn down your grandmother?'

'The merest bagatelle,' Erasmus murmurs.

'Then it's as well I don't require any more of you than this,' says Kitty: 'that you go on letting me cocoon you in lies, like a spider wrapping its silk around a fly.'

'Ah, Kitty, Kitty!' Erasmus groans. 'What wouldn't I give for one of your kisses?'

Kitty sniggers, and for the briefest of seconds, the tip of her soot-black tongue shows between her teeth.

'Impetuous fool!' she says. 'A kiss from me would poach your brains and send them dribbling out through your ears. It's better to be tantalized than toasted.'

The small portion of Erasmus's intellect that is capable of functioning independently asserts itself.

'I'm worried about Lord Bortle,' he confides. 'We must keep him sweet. If he goes blabbing about the League of the Golden Unicorn, the jig will be up.'

Kitty huffs and stamps like a cab-horse.

'You're going to be serious again, I can tell!' she snaps. 'You're going to deliver one of your interminable lectures about rights, and duties, and causes. You don't care for me in the slightest, Erasmus Slike. I'm simply a plaything to you, a trivial piece on the gaming board of your ambition.'

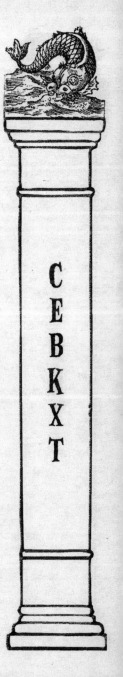

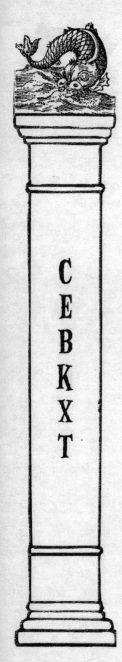

Erasmus places his right hand over his heart.

'My dear, when the game is done, yours is the only cause I shall seek to follow,' he says sincerely. 'My devotion to you will be entire – body, mind and soul.'

Kitty shrugs.

'To be candid, your body and mind don't interest me,' she says. 'But your soul? Mm, that affords me hundreds of fascinating prospects!'

She grants Erasmus the reward of a smile.

Encouraged by the apparent improvement in Kitty's mood, Erasmus gingerly returns to the subject of the irascible aristocrat.

'It was you who brought the Fabulary Garden to the league's attention, Kitty,' he reminds her. 'You suggested the bargain that we struck with Lord Bortle. He has my word, and we really ought to give him his werewolf.'

Kitty narrows her eyes.

'Then give him some advice, and tell him that he must learn to be patient!' she hisses. 'He can't have what he wants the instant that he wants it, so he'll have to wait. His lordship has the mentality of a stamp-collector. He understands nothing about the creatures he keeps in captivity. He is entirely ignorant of their needs, their gnawing longing for the worlds from which they were ripped.'

Erasmus is taken aback. He has never heard Kitty speak with such passion. Is her lower lip quivering with outrage? Can that be a sympathetic tear welling up in her left eye?

'I am familiar with the ways of demons; you and Lord Bortle are not,' Kitty continues. 'In dealings with those of a lycanthropic persuasion, it behoves one to make optimum use of the lunar cycle.'

Erasmus's face is the very picture of bafflement.

'Eh?' he grunts.

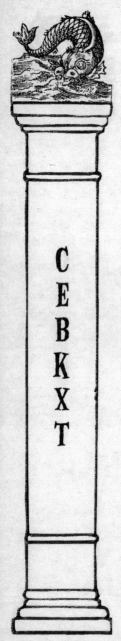

C
E
B
K
X
T

'Werewolves are best handled on nights when the moon is full,' Kitty explains. 'Offer him some advice instead, and tell him that his specimen will be delivered within three days.'

Meanwhile, a rather awkward breakfast is in progress at Scarlatti Mews. Callisto is not yet up, so Dessica Flaunt has had to introduce herself to Mrs Moncrief, Aril and Crispin. The three youngsters are currently seated around a table laden with a tureen of porridge, a pot of tea, a pot of coffee, a jug of milk, a platter of kippers, two racks of toast, a dish of butter, and jars containing an assortment of condiments and conserves.

Dessica eats in nervous nibbles, her eyes constantly darting from side to side. She has gained a mixed impression of her hosts. Mrs Moncrief, she regards as cracked, but kindly. Aril's grace and beauty have awed her.

Got to be royalty, thinks Dessica. Maharajah's daughter at least.

And there is something else about Aril. One afternoon, having gained illicit entry to the Bickerstaffe Zoological Gardens, Dessica passed a delightful hour watching a lioness tend her cubs. Aril reminds her of that lioness: she seems to possess the same restrained power.

Crispin strikes Dessica as far less complicated. He has a likeable enough face. His clothes are smart, but he does not talk poshly. He has a marked accent, which Dessica is blessed if she can place. As cautiously as a snail emerging from its shell after a sudden fright, she turns to Crispin and says, 'What part of Wolveston are you from?'

'No part,' says Crispin. 'I'm from London.'

'London – where's that then?'

Crispin swallows a spoonful of milky porridge.

C
E
B
K
X
T

C
E
B
K
X
T

'Down south,' he says.

'What's London like?'

'Dump,' says Crispin.

Aril gives Dessica a smile that would light a candle.

'What do you do, Dessica?' she enquires.

'I'm a river girl,' says Dessica. 'I mostly row up and down the Bast at night and take stuff off any floaters I find – that's the bodies of suicides,' she adds helpfully. 'Otherwise, I cheat a bit, nick a bit, whatever it takes.'

'Whatever it takes to do what?' says Crispin.

'Keep alive,' Dessica says. 'Don't worry, I won't nick nothing off either of you. You're all right.'

'Not completely,' says Aril, and once more Dessica senses that Aril is keeping a secret.

Crispin has a question so urgent that it has set him jiggling. 'Don't you ever get scared, touching dead bodies?'

'Floaters can't hurt you,' Dessica says. 'It's the living you got to watch out for. I'm here on account of a floater. I found a notebook in the pocket of a dead bloke last night, took it to show Squalida MacHeath, and she sent me off with Callisto.'

Crispin grins nostalgically.

'Squalida MacHeath!' he sighs. 'She took me prisoner once, and locked me in a crypt. Lucky for me, Aril turned into a— ow!'

Crispin convulses, then bends down to give his right shin a vigourous rub.

'I'm so sorry, Crispin!' Aril apologizes sweetly. 'Did my foot slip?'

Before Crispin can respond, the door opens and Callisto sweeps in. The magician's brows are knitted, his jaw is firm, his eyes are at their gravest.

'Good morning,' he says. 'I have an announcement to make. It's come to my attention that Wolveston is no longer a

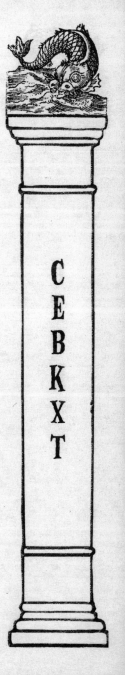

C
E
B
K
X
T

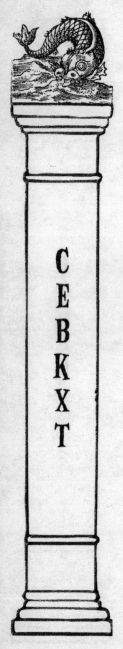

safe location for people of your age. Consequently, I have decided to send the three of you to France with Mrs Moncrief. I'll make the bookings after breakfast, and you will leave this afternoon. I intend to remain in Wolveston, and counter the danger alone.'

Chapter Nine:
Togetherness

The response to Callisto's proposal is immediate.

With considerable emphasis Aril says, 'No!'

'Not blumming likely!' cries Crispin.

'I ain't going nowhere!' mutters Dessica. 'I ain't going to no France. They eat slugs over there.'

'Snails,' Callisto corrects her.

Dessica cocks an eyebrow at him. 'And that's better, is it?'

Callisto's frown deepens.

'Come, come!' he insists. 'This is no time for an act of defiance.'

Aril folds her arms.

'This is *exactly* the time for defiance!'

Y
K
R
Q
O
K

she boldly informs her guardian. 'This is one of those harebrained ideas that you haven't thought through properly.'

'Haven't I?' says Callisto, sounding less than confident.

'Of course you haven't,' says Aril. 'Take me for instance. A full moon is due. How will I cope with it in France? Do French ironmongers stock the right kinds of chains and padlocks, or will I have to take my own with me? And if I do, how will I account for them if a customs officer searches my luggage?'

Dessica catches Crispin's eye, and mouths, 'Chains and padlocks?'

Crispin closes his eyes and shakes his head to indicate that it is not a convenient moment to go into details.

'Ah!' says Callisto. 'Well, um, I, er—'

'And what if we'd left you alone with my barmy Uncle Jasper last year?' Crispin interrupts. 'How would you have managed then, eh?'

'Well,' says Callisto, 'er, admittedly, I would have—'

To the surprise of all, Mrs Moncrief suddenly bounds into the room, brandishing a fully-extended toasting-fork.

'And, pray, where would you have been without my cab-driving skills?' she demands.

'Cab-driving?' Dessica says silently to Crispin, who closes his eyes and shakes his head again.

'Yes,' concedes Callisto, 'your assistance was most opportune, but—' He breaks off and looks askance at the housekeeper. 'Mrs M, were you listening in to this private conversation?'

Mrs Moncrief draws herself up to her full height.

'Listen in?' she declaims haughtily. 'I am no spy, Mr Callisto. I listened to nothing, I merely chanced to overhear.'

'Instead of ordering us about, why don't you tell us the facts and let us decide for

YKRQOK

Y
K
R
Q
O
K

ourselves?' suggests Aril. 'It's not as if we're children.'

Callisto knows better than to contradict this assertion. He is clearly outnumbered, and well and truly snookered. Raising both hands in a gesture of surrender, he says, 'All right, but I would still rest easier if—'

'Explain!' commands Aril.

And so Callisto reveals what he has discovered about the League of the Golden Unicorn, the plot to restore the monarchy, and the deadly beast that is at large in the Scarp.

Most of what he says passes over Dessica's head. She is not much concerned about martial law and the overthrow of governments. Kings and queens, she holds, are a pretty rotten bunch taken all in all. This conviction was instilled in her by Nelly Boot, who taught her such nursery rhymes as:

Lavender's blue, dilly dilly,
Poppies are red,
When I am king, dilly dilly,
I'll be shot dead.

The king and queen went to the green
To fetch a pail of water.
They both fell down and broke their
  crowns,
And the people were happier after.

What greatly concerns Dessica is the atmosphere in the room. Since Nelly died, Dessica has thought only of herself. In her struggle for survival, she has eschewed any form of friendship, and even her acquaintances are few and far between. But here in Scarlatti Mews, she is keenly aware of the togetherness that links Callisto, Aril, Crispin and Mrs Moncrief, and she wonders whether she has missed out on something. Dessica senses the closeness of the trust around her, and while she is not

Y
K
R
Q
O
K

exactly envious, she catches herself wishing that she could earn a share of it.

Callisto concludes his exposition.

'What's your plan?' asks Aril.

'Scrappy,' Callisto confesses. 'First, I must try and put an end to the activities of the murderous beast that is terrifying the Scarp. Hopefully, it will prevent the widespread rioting that the League of the Golden Unicorn is depending on to weaken and then destroy Parliament. After that, I'm undecided.'

'What d'you reckon the beast is, Mr Callisto?' says Crispin.

Callisto seems discomforted. He glances furtively at Dessica, and blushes. 'I, er, think that I should postpone my response to that question until—'

'It's me, ain't it?' Dessica says. 'You don't want to say nothing in front of me, because I'm an outsider. Well let me tell you something, Callisto. Whatever this thing is, it's killing my sort of people, and

I want to help stop it. I've lived in the Scarp all my life, and I can find my way round it like none of you lot can. Before you can deal with the beast, you got to find it, and that's where I come in. So what we looking for?'

Callisto heaves a sigh.

'Very well, Dessica,' he says resignedly, 'but I must warn you that what you are about to hear may be profoundly shocking. It may cause you to doubt those fundamental beliefs which, until now, you have taken for granted. It will seize the flimsy veil of reality and—'

'Get on with it!' pleads Dessica.

'To put it directly then,' says Callisto, 'this world of ours is occasionally visited by beings who are popularly termed . . . demons.'

'I know,' says Dessica, with a shrug.

Callisto is astounded.

'You *know*?' he gasps. 'How can you possibly know?'

Y K R Q O K

'Keep my eyes open, don't I?' Dessica replies nonchalantly. 'There's more than people walking the Scarp at night. What kind of demon are we talking about?'

'I'm not yet certain, but with any luck I will have settled the matter by this evening,' Callisto says. 'In order to do that, I must visit an old colleague of mine. In the meantime, Mrs Moncrief, I would be obliged if you, Aril and Crispin would go to the Reference Section of the National Library, consult the Army Register, and find out all you can about Captain Carlton Maroon and the First Wolveston Lancers.'

'Certainly, Mr Callisto,' says Mrs Moncrief.

'And what about me?' Dessica enquires.

'You may accompany them, or stay here if you prefer,' Callisto says.

'No fear!' says Dessica. 'I'm coming with you, Callisto!'

Callisto subjects her to a severe look.

'I hope you're not going to give me any trouble,' he says.

Dessica opens her eyes as wide as she can.

'Trouble – me?' she says in an offended tone. 'I'm sure I don't know what you mean!'

For some years, a section of what was once the south transept of St Augustine's cathedral in Gospelmaker Road has done Squalida MacHeath service as a map room. Occupying an enormous table in the centre of the room is a scale model of Wolveston, sculpted in clay and painted in painstaking detail. Squalida MacHeath stands brooding over the model, looking like a particularly succulent humbug in her black-and-white striped dress. Two men are with her: Mr Penniweather, her Chief Book-keeper, and Mr Kolakis, one of her advisers.

Mr Penniweather's pate is glossily bald,

Y
K
R
Q
O
K

YKRQOK

and to compensate, he has teased out the grey hair at the sides of his head into two pointed cones that resemble a pair of coconut macaroons. His eyes are hidden behind the blue-tinted lenses of his spectacles. He is reciting a list of the previous night's takings in a fittingly doleful voice.

'Bare-knuckle fighting, down sixty-one per cent,' he intones. 'Public houses, down twenty per cent. Betting parlours, down fifty-two per cent. Opium dens, down seventeen per cent . . .'

The list, it seems, goes on and ever on.

Mr Kolakis is tall, well-proportioned and dapper. He wears a light-grey silk suit, a gold brocade waistcoat, a pale-yellow cravat and white spats over black patent-leather shoes. His tightly curled black hair is so shiny that it too might be made of patent leather. He has an olive complexion, thoughtful brown eyes and a sensitive mouth. Of Greek extraction, if Mr Kolakis lived in the time of his distant forebears, someone would undoubtedly have raised a temple for him. His neighbours in Highside assume that he is a respectable stockbroker; in fact he is a criminal mastermind, and Squalida employs him because she is apprehensive about how well he might fare if he employed himself.

Mr Kolakis is currently engaged in pinning a number of red paper flags on the model of the city.

'Thank you, Mr Penniweather, that is as much financial news as I can stand!' says Squalida. 'How much have I lost in total?'

'More than you can afford,' Mr Penniweather answers.

'Any advice?'

Mr Penniweather adjusts his spectacles so that they sit more comfortably on the bridge of his nose.

'Take a holiday in the South Sea Isles, and forget to come back,' he says.

Squalida smiles.

'Tempting, but I'm not done yet,' she says. 'You can go now.'

Mr Penniweather leaves, and Squalida turns her attention to Mr Kolakis.

'Well, Pantalis, what has your clever brain deduced?'

Mr Kolakis takes his chin between the thumb and index finger of his left hand.

'These flags mark the places where the bodies were found,' he says.

'Highly decorative, to be sure, but does it tell us anything?'

'The vast majority are within half a mile of the Bast,' says Mr Kolakis. 'The killer likes the river.'

'He owns a boat!' Squalida exclaims.

'Or perhaps he is fond of swimming,' says Mr Kolakis.

Chapter Ten:
Mechanisms

This is the famous Reading Room of the National Library in Threeble Street. It is circular, and operates as the hub of the building. From its circumference radiate aisles that run between tall shelves. The walls of the Reading Room are crowded with books. Standing here and there on slender plinths are busts of history's finest literary geniuses: Homer, Virgil, Dante, Chaucer, Shakespeare and Dafydd ap Gwilym, among others.

The room's tables and chairs have been upholstered in dark-green leather. Many of the tables are occupied, predominantly by elderly scholars who

wear pince-nez and sport bushy white beards, like toy poodles clinging to their faces.

Mrs Moncrief, Aril and Crispin stand on one side of the enquiries counter; on the other side stands a librarian. His hair is grey, as are his eyes, skin, shirt, tie, suit and shoes.

The librarian speaks in a voice as dry as dust, apparently without moving his lips. 'How may I be of service, madam?'

Mrs Moncrief cups one hand beside her mouth and says, in the exaggerated whisper of an actress playing a dowager in a drawing-room comedy, 'Would you kindly direct my companions and myself to the Reference Section?'

'I'm sorry, but the Reference Section is closed for refurbishment,' says the librarian. 'If you would let me know which titles you require, I'll fetch them up from the stack-room.'

Mrs Moncrief leans closer, and whispers more loudly, 'I wish to consult the Army Register.'

The librarian manifests signs of agitation. His Adam's apple bobs. A nervous tic troubles the corner of his mouth.

'The Army Register runs to thirty-seven volumes, madam,' he says. 'Could you be more specific about your area of interest?'

'I wish to peruse the annals of the First Wolveston Lancers!' declares Mrs Moncrief.

The librarian quails visibly. Grey beads of sweat stand out on his forehead.

'C-certainly, m-madam,' he stammers. 'If you would just f-fill in this f-form, I'll f-fetch the relevant volume at once.'

He places a sheet of paper and a pencil on the counter, turns, scoots over to the entrance of an aisle, and disappears.

'He was a bit jumpy, wasn't he?' remarks Crispin.

Without looking up from the form she is completing, Mrs Moncrief says, 'One can

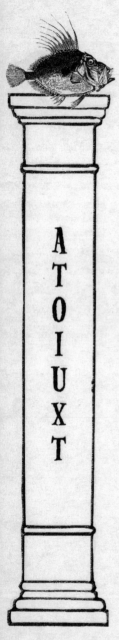

only presume that he was disconcerted by my femininity.'

'He wasn't disconcerted,' murmurs Aril. 'He was frightened.'

The irises of her eyes swirl as their colour changes from brown to tawny-yellow.

The grey librarian ducks down a side-aisle, and seeks out a shelf of rarely consulted books which detail the history of cheese manufacture in Iceland. Concealed behind two of the books is a miniature telegraph device, fixed to a metal plate on a hinged arm. The librarian swings out the plate, reaches for the key of the telegraph, and taps out a message.

```
      REQUEST RECEIVED FOR ARMY
   REGISTER FIRST WOLVESTON LANCERS
      - STOP - PLEASE ADVISE -
            TRANSMISSION ENDS
```

The librarian has been issued with strict instructions, but he is not following them willingly. Should he fail to comply, a document detailing the rare volumes that he has stolen from the library and sold for his own profit will be sent to the authorities, which will result in his spending a long stretch in Rollaway Prison. He awaits a reply in an agonized ecstasy.

At last, the telegraph receiver ticks. The librarian listens intently.

PROVIDE DETAILS OF REQUESTER
AT EARLIEST OPPORTUNITY –
TRANSMISSION ENDS

It has been a long while since Dessica Flaunt travelled on the Wolveston Subterranean Railway whilst in possession of a valid ticket, and she finds her licit journey somewhat staid and lacking in excitement. Callisto is in the seat next to hers, and she keeps stealing sideways looks at him. His presence is oddly reassuring, and Dessica feels secure enough

A T O I U X T

to indulge in a little tactful interrogation.

'Aril your daughter then?' she demands abruptly.

'No, she is my ward,' explains Callisto. 'I'm her guardian.'

'You Crispin's guardian and all?'

'No,' says Callisto. 'Crispin is an orphan. His late mother, Rachel, was a dear friend of mine.'

Dessica nudges Callisto's arm with her elbow.

'You and her were sweethearts, eh?' she teases.

Callisto's only response is a cool blink.

'It was the way you said her name,' says Dessica, by way of apology. 'I'm good at noticing stuff like that.'

'I'll be sure to remember,' says Callisto.

'Is there a Mrs Callisto tucked away somewhere?'

'Yes, in the distant future,' says Callisto. 'I've not yet had the good fortune to make her acquaintance.'

Dessica judges that a rapid change of subject is called for.

'Where we off to?' she asks.

'To the Taft Institute in Daedalus Square, to consult with my old friend Evaricus Tinsley, who is professor of the Experimental Department.'

'Coo!' Dessica exclaims. 'How come you know him then?'

Callisto shrugs. 'It's a common enough story. In his youth, Evaricus won a scholarship to Lardus College, Cambridge, to study Mathematics, Mythology and Machinery. Unfortunately, he was caught dallying with the provost's daughter, and was punished with a year's rustication. Instead of languishing in disgrace, Evaricus taught himself fire-eating, and joined Balthasar Bright's Travelling Circus, where I was employed as a conjuror. We became friends, and have remained friends since. Evaricus has designed several ingenious pieces of apparatus for my stage act.'

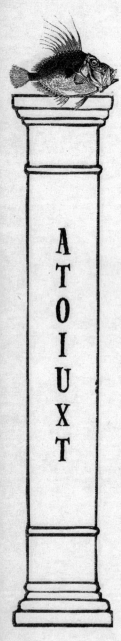

'Sounds a clever sort of bloke,' Dessica says.

'He is one of the most brilliant people in the country,' concurs Callisto.

Dessica reflects on her situation. A little over twelve hours ago, she was fishing a corpse from the Bast; now she is mixing with stage stars and eminent professors.

'Funny old life, ain't it?' she muses aloud.

Callisto fails to appreciate the comment's significance.

The Taft Institute for Engineering, Mechanics and Invention, to give it its full title, was first housed in a building so unassuming as to go largely unnoticed. Its architect was Daniel Taft himself, who drafted his plans with functionality rather than decorativeness in mind, and the main block resembles a red-brick shoe-box with a mansard roof of blueish slate. A number of annexes have been added over the years, each carefully echoing the innocuous style of the original edifice. Within the institute's lecture halls and laboratories, theories are propounded, discoveries are made, and innovations are rigorously tested. It was here that the renowned Rufus Cobbleday constructed the first Steam Staircase, and Phillida Spendlove developed the prototype of her Self-Inflating Girdle, which has kept the paws of many an old sea dog out of a watery grave.

Callisto presents himself at the Reception Office, and as soon as he mentions his name, the porter on duty pipes up, 'Ah, yes, Mr Callisto! Professor Tinsley told me to tell you that you'll find him in Block E Two, which lies between Block E One and Block E Three.' The porter taps a finger against the side of his nose and adds, 'The bicycling team is with him.'

'Capital!' says Callisto.

As she walks with Callisto along the gravel path that joins the annexes, Dessica

cannot help feeling intimidated by the institute's ambience.

'What do people get up to here, Callisto?' she says.

'Thinking, mostly,' Callisto replies.

'Can you make a living out of thinking then?'

'If you have the right thoughts,' Callisto says.

Dessica walks a few more paces, and then the question she is burning to ask bursts forth from her. 'A *bicycling* team?'

'All will be made clear in time,' Callisto assures her.

They turn aside, and walk towards a building that has E2 painted in large red characters on its front door. The door opens as they approach, and a man wearing a white overall emerges.

'Callisto!' he cries.

'Evaricus!' returns Callisto.

While the two friends shake hands and slap each other on the back, Dessica takes a good hard look at the first professor she has knowingly encountered. He is not what she was expecting.

On the very few occasions when she has thought about a professor, Dessica has pictured a white-haired old gentleman, cackling insanely as he pours luridly coloured liquids into a glass beaker whose contents bubble and smoke.

Evaricus Tinsley is in his early forties, and is clean-shaven. His hair is blond, and neatly brushed. An inclination to overindulgence is apparent in his slightly pudgy features, but he is handsome after a boyish fashion. He fixes his cornflower-blue eyes on Dessica and says, 'Who is this bewitching creature?'

'Ain't no witch!' snarls Dessica.

'This is Miss Flaunt,' Callisto says. 'She is currently a guest at Scarlatti Mews.'

'Not for long though,' says Dessica. 'Soon as I find a crib that suits me, I'm off, matey!'

A T O I U X T

ATOIUXT

'I admire your independent spirit, Miss Flaunt,' Evaricus says, bowing gallantly. He grins at Callisto. 'Your telegram mentioned a conundrum?'

'That it did,' confirms Callisto. 'I wonder if it will prove too much for your infernal device. The last time you gave me a demonstration, as I recall, it took almost an hour to calculate the square root of nine.'

Evaricus guffaws at the memory.

'I think we can do better than that now!' he says. 'We've made great strides in the last six months. What's the nature of your conundrum?'

'I'm seeking to identify a demon,' says Callisto.

Evaricus does not balk at the revelation. Though he is a scientist by profession and inclination, he is aware that science has its limitations, and in Callisto's company he has had experiences that went far beyond the reach of logic.

'Let's see what we can do for you, shall we?' he offers.

Evaricus steps over to the door, opens it, ushers Callisto and Dessica inside, then enters E Block himself.

'Callisto, Miss Flaunt, meet the new and improved Compendium Engine!' he announces proudly.

Dessica stares and stares.

'Cremola!' she gasps.

The dimensions of the Compendium Engine are such that it would fill the auditorium of a modestly sized Italian opera house. It is comprised of countless brass cogwheels, and square-sectioned steel rods; chains, wires and drive-belts stretch like sinews within its frame. In front of it stands a long panel festooned with dials, buttons, knobs, switches, and more levers than a railway signal-box. The engine glints and gleams, and smells of oil and ozone.

To one side, bolted to a thick brass rail,

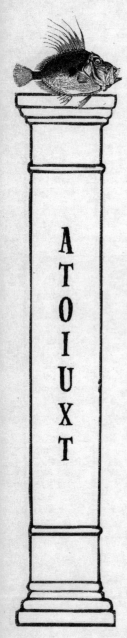

A T O I U X T

are what appear to be four bicycles whose front wheels have been removed. The back wheels are attached to nickelled-silver chains, which are attached in turn to four large metal discs, set facing one another at a distance of a few centimetres.

'It's beautiful!' says Dessica. 'What's it do?'

'It turns questions into numbers, and does calculations,' Evaricus says, 'many hundreds of calculations simultaneously. If human beings were to essay the task, they would soon grow bored and tired, and they would make mistakes. The Compendium Engine needs no rest and cannot be distracted. Once its calculations are complete, it answers the question.'

'You mean it's a machine what *thinks*?' squeaks Dessica.

Evaricus is rather taken with her reaction, and he smiles.

'Not exactly,' he says, 'but that's rather a good way of putting it. I salute your way with words, Miss Flaunt.'

'Don't you come the charmer with me!' Dessica growls.

'I'll just set the engine to demon phase,' Evaricus informs Callisto, then proceeds to flick switches and throw levers. Ratchets clack like chattering magpies, flywheels turn, gyroscopes revolve, gears engage.

'That's it!' says Evaricus. 'What data have you brought us, Callisto?'

Callisto reaches into his jacket and withdraws a notebook containing jottings that he made shortly after his interview with the mortician, Mr Spaughm.

'Details of wounds found on the bodies of the demon's victims,' he says. 'Depth and length of lacerations, bite radii, extent and severity of burns.'

'Burns?' says Evaricus. 'That should narrow down the field. Fire away!'

Callisto reads out the information; Evaricus turns knobs, adjusts dials,

presses buttons. When all is to his satisfaction, the master of the Compendium Engine crosses to a copper mouthpiece attached to the panel, removes a stopper from it, and says, 'We are ready for you, gentlemen.'

Almost at once, from somewhere in the building comes the sound of an opening door, and the tramp of marching feet. From around the side of the engine stride four men, dressed in matching straw boaters, full-length bathing costumes striped in blue and yellow, and white canvas shoes. They all have brown hair, sweeping moustaches and muscular physiques.

'Callisto, Miss Flaunt,' says Evaricus, 'allow me to present the Taft Institute's Bicycling Team.'

As one, the team's members doff their hats, and replace them on their heads.

'To your places, gentlemen,' Evaricus says.

The team mounts the row of strange

bicycles, and begins to pedal. The metal discs attached to the back wheels spin counter to one another.

A gnat-like whine swells to a sonorous hum. Minuscule bolts of lightning crackle between the spinning discs, and the Compendium Engine springs to life. Cog wheels purr as contentedly as recently fed cats. Steel rods rise and fall, producing the illusion of a lazily undulating ocean. Chains snick, and swap from one cog to another.

After perhaps ten minutes, Evaricus raises his left hand. The pumping legs of the cyclists slow to a stop, and so does the great machine at their backs. The men dismount, raise their staw boaters and make their exit.

Accompanied by a burst of staccato clicks, a length of paper tape is exuded from a slot in the panel. Evaricus tears off the tape, examines it, and says, 'Draco sinesis.'

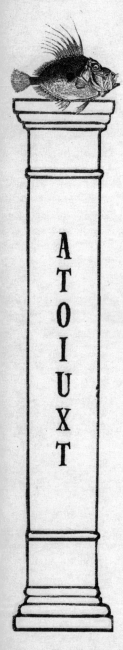

Callisto's face turns pale.

'Dray whatsis?' says Dessica.

Callisto's voice is hoarse.

'The demon in the Scarp is a Chinese dragon,' he says.

Chapter Eleven:
In High Places

As the members of the Taft Institute's Bicycling Team mop their brows and catch their breaths following their exertions on the Compendium Engine, on the opposite side of the Channel, Paris is resplendent in the glorious summer sunshine that has followed hard on the heels of a rainy squall. The wet rooftops and cobbled streets of the city shine as if they have been newly gilded.

On the rue de Richelieu, reflected light bounces up into the windows of the first-floor apartment, where Mariah Stuart is receiving a visitor.

Throughout history there have been many pretenders to the throne of Greater

Britain, but none has pretended to it more prettily than Mariah. She is in her early twenties, and has brown hair, a smooth complexion, eyes of an arresting blue, a delicate nose and a Cupid's-bow mouth. Her brown dress is simple – 'severe' some might call it – for she does not seek to emulate the frills, furbelows, paints and powders of the fashionable ladies-about-town. A keen intelligence and a thorough education have afforded her mastery of at least a dozen languages. Close study of the personal history of her ancestors, a sorry chronicle of dashed hopes and broken promises, has left her sceptical. Her gaze is ironically detached; her wit is drier than a desert lizard.

Mariah's visitor is aged and rotund. His flabby, chinless features are turtle-like. He is none other than the archbishop who attended the meeting of the League of the Golden Unicorn at the Fairfax Club. The archbishop has exchanged his priestly regalia for a plain, if beautifully tailored, dark-blue suit. He bows low.

'Your majesty!' he burbles.

'I am not your majesty just yet,' Mariah points out. 'I prefer to be called "Miss Stuart", your grace.'

The archbishop beams at her – an unnerving sight.

'And since I am travelling incognito, perhaps it would be more appropriate for you to address me as "Mr Parrock",' he oozes.

Mariah motions to a nearby armchair.

'Please take a seat, Mr Parrock,' she says. 'Why have you called on me?'

The archbishop shuffles to accommodate his not inconsiderable posterior, and says, 'I am on an errand of mercy, Miss Stuart. Mr Slike has led me to understand that you are undergoing a dark night of the soul, a spiritual crisis occasioned by qualms concerning the intentions of the League of the Golden Unicorn.'

'Mr Slike is mistaken, Mr Parrock,' retorts

M X E V N U T

Mariah. 'I have no qualms, I have doubts. I'm not entirely sure that I want to be queen.'

The archbishop's cheeks flap like the whites of two frying eggs.

'*Not want to be queen?*' he splutters. 'My dear young woman, the sacred office of monarchy was ordained by the Almighty Himself. Kings and queens are His representatives on Earth.'

'I'm not clear as to why the Almighty – who is, it stands to reason, all-mighty – needs to have representatives,' muses Mariah. 'But please, don't enlighten me. Supposing I agree to be crowned, how would that sit with my beliefs?'

The archbishop is mystified.

'I beg your pardon, Miss Stuart?' he says.

'I am a Catholic,' says Mariah. 'Surely a Catholic can't be Supreme Head of the Church of Greater Britain?'

The archbishop titters merrily, and pats his palms against his knees.

'Have no fears on that count, Miss Stuart!' he gurgles. 'The Church of Greater Britain has nothing to do with religion, and very little to do with belief. It is a comfortable Sunday club, where the lower orders go to have their guilt refreshed, and the well-to-do go to have their superiority reinforced. Being a spiritual leader need not trouble your conscience one whit – I know that being a spiritual leader has never troubled mine.'

'But innocent people are being killed because of me!' Mariah protests. 'That can't be right in the Almighty's Eyes.'

The archbishop puffs as he frantically casts about for a scrap of justification.

'Dear Miss Stuart, the tenderness of your heart does you great credit,' he asserts at last, 'but who is truly innocent in this Vale of Tears? With each second that ticks by, people die meaningless deaths. Those who die on your account

M
X
E
V
N
U
T

are dying for a purpose. You have granted the gift of significance to their demise!'

Mariah remains unmoved by the archbishop's argument. The truth is that she has begun to feel trapped by circumstances, and the prospect of becoming a monarch fills her with panic and loathing. She has pictured the tedium that will haunt her days: the unremitting cycle of meetings with dignitaries, courtiers and politicians; the eternal succession of banquets held in honour of foreign heads of state who have no desire to be honoured, and who will find the process as pointless and stultifying as she will herself. The public and press will continually hound her. Protocol will rigidly dictate how she behaves, what she wears, where she goes and whom she sees, and in order to submit to the boredom and inconsequence of monarchy, she must give up Paris and freedom.

Mariah flashes a smile of sensational

insincerity and says, 'Thank you so much for dropping by, Mr Parrock. I can't begin to tell you how much consolation you have brought me. Your wisdom has helped me to decide upon my proper course of action. I hope that the next time we meet, you will be able to stay a little longer.'

The archbishop smirks, then realizes that what he took purely as a compliment was also intended to be a signal for him to depart.

He bumbles to his feet and bows again.

'I pray that, in future, you will regard me as a father confessor, Miss Stuart,' he says.

Mariah, who regards him as a pompous hypocrite, makes no reply.

Since his startling consultation with Evaricus Tinsley and the Compendium Engine, Callisto has been so rapt in thought that Dessica Flaunt has refrained

M X E V N U T

from disturbing him. However, as they leave Bywater Station and proceed along Eden Road, en route to Scarlatti Mews, her forbearance comes to an end.

'How the blue did a dragon get from China to Wolveston?' she exclaims.

'It didn't,' says Callisto. 'Chinese dragons don't come from China.'

'Then where the Rowley do they come from?'

Callisto sighs.

'It's difficult to explain,' he says.

'Oh, well don't even bother trying!' snaps Dessica. 'I'm only an ignorant river girl, so I couldn't possibly understand, could I?'

Callisto is suitably chastened.

'I apologize for being condescending,' he says humbly. 'Bear with me while I attempt to describe simply a situation which is, quite literally, fiendishly complicated. Dragons, both Chinese and Northern, live in demon worlds.'

'Inferno?'

'Quite so, but this is where the complication begins,' Callisto says. 'Inferno is not strictly speaking a world, but rather a junction point where myriad worlds, including ours, intersect. Mythical animals are not a myth, but the inhabitants of these other worlds.'

'With you so far!' chirrups Dessica. 'How did the dragon get here?'

Callisto absently tugs at the lobe of his left ear.

'Sometimes the barriers between the worlds wear thin, and something passes through from one reality to another, but I don't believe that applies in this instance,' he says. 'Captain Maroon's notebook hints that someone has been collecting fauna from the demon worlds, and placing them in some sort of zoo.'

Dessica laughs nervously.

'Who'd want to do a stupid thing like that?' she says.

'Someone with enormous wealth,' opines Callisto. 'Someone who has the time and space to devote to such an enterprise.'

'A toff!' Dessica cries.

Callisto is impressed by her deductive powers.

'That's just what I have been thinking,' he says. 'But one thing troubles me greatly.'

'What?'

'Chinese dragons are timid, benevolent creatures,' says Callisto. 'They are the bringers of gentle rain and warm winds. What can have transformed the dragon in the Scarp into a killer?'

As Callisto and Dessica leave Eden Road and enter Pinchbeck Street, Dessica puts herself in the dragon's place.

'Maybe it's homesick,' she proposes. 'Maybe it wants to go back where it belongs, but it can't. Maybe it's lonely, and miserable, and everyone who meets it is scared of it, and it doesn't know why, so it gets scared back, and lashes out.'

Callisto arches his right eyebrow.

'You are a most surprising young person, Dessica Flaunt,' he says.

Dessica grimaces.

'Regular little jack-in-the-box, ain't I?' she mutters.

Upon her employer's return to Scarlatti Mews, Mrs Moncrief serves up a sumptuous luncheon. While it is being partaken of, Callisto shares the knowledge he gained at the Taft Institute, and simultaneously sorts through the mail that was delivered in his absence. Amidst the customary crop of perfumed, pastel-coloured envelopes, sent, for the most part, by admiring female fans, is a telegram which Callisto reads aloud.

'*Killer moves about on, or in, the Bast – Squalida.*'

Instantly, Dessica recalls the giant goldfish of Wolveston.

'I saw it last night, about ten o'clock!'

MXEVNUT

M
X
E
V
N
U
T

she gasps. 'It was swimming east, near Three Rivals Wharf.'

'That information may well prove useful,' conjectures Callisto. 'What luck with the Army Register, Crispin?'

Crispin produces a page of carefully compiled notes, and reads from it. 'Carlton Maroon attended military college in Oswestry. After passing out as a lieutenant, he served seven years in garrisons along the Great Eastern Canal, and was promoted to captain a month before his posting to Toolham, where his Commanding Officer was Brigadier Plumpton Drury. Brigadier Drury was awarded the Protector's Medal for his part in the Crimean Famine Relief campaign, in which he served under Field Marshal Sir Jarvis Barkshaw.'

Commanding Officer – CO! thinks Callisto. FM – Field Marshal!

He is convinced that he has identified two of the shadowy individuals mentioned in Captain Maroon's notebook, but the discovery is no cause for celebration.

'Senior military personnel are involved with the League of the Golden Unicorn,' he speculates. 'And who else? How far does the conspiracy stretch? It's possible that members of the government may be implicated.' He shakes his head. 'Tackling a rogue Chinese dragon is one thing; tackling treason in high places is quite another. Whom could I trust with what I know?'

Dessica does not hear Callisto's final question, for she is too intent on Aril.

Something untoward is taking place. Aril's hair whips this way and that, as if wind-blown, but there is no wind in the room. Ominous bumps gather on her knuckles, disappear and then gather again. The pupils of her eyes have changed shape from circles to vertical slits.

'You feeling all right, Aril?' Dessica asks.

Aril quivers; her voice judders as she

M
X
E
V
N
U
T

M
X
E
V
N
U
T

says, 'The moon! The moon is coming!'

Dessica turns in alarm to Crispin. 'What's wrong with her?'

'You don't know us well enough to be told,' says Crispin.

It is the first rebuff that Dessica has met with since her arrival in Scarlatti Mews, and she is surprised how deeply her feelings are hurt by it, but she does not remain offended for long.

'Go up to your room and lie down, Aril,' Callisto instructs his ward. 'I'll ask Mrs Moncrief to sit with you.'

Aril withdraws without demur.

'This evening, Dessica, you will accompany Crispin and myself to the Egyptian Theatre,' Callisto resumes. 'After the performance, you will act as our guide to the byways of the Scarp. We are going dragon hunting.'

Chapter Twelve:
A Siren Stone

Erasmus Slike and Kitty Montez are paying a visit to Steyne House in an attempt to placate Lord Bortle. The earl was frostily taciturn upon their arrival, but since then Kitty has coaxed, cajoled and flirted him out of his fit of the sulks. Erasmus, however, remains in disgrace, and Lord Bortle ignores him.

Kitty, arm in arm with the earl, has been shown around the Fabulary Garden. Lord Bortle has been so full of himself, boasting of the expenditure he laid out to acquire his exhibits, that he has failed to notice the little telltale signs in the demeanour of his entrancing companion. Kitty's jaw muscles are tightly bunched,

QXGQKT

her lips are compressed into a thin line, her eyes flash angrily. Beneath the coolness of her voice something writhes and rages.

Lord Bortle, Kitty and Erasmus are standing beside a circular embankment whose steeply sloping sides surround a pool in which an Afanc, an animal somewhere between a giant beaver and a crocodile, floats torpidly in murky water. The only parts of the Afanc which are visible are the scaly crest of its spine, its nostrils, and its bereft brown eyes.

'And so you see, Miss Montez,' Lord Bortle says waggishly, 'one paid a pretty penny for an ugly brute!'

Kitty smiles dutifully.

'Personally, I wouldn't go so far as to call it ugly, my lord,' she declares. 'I expect that, to another of its kind, this Afanc is the loveliest creature in Creation.'

Lord Bortle's forehead corrugates into a frown.

'Too philosophical for me!' he grunts. 'Look here, Miss Montez, you're not deep, are you?'

Kitty's laugh is light, bewitching; false.

'My lord, I am as shallow as the upper layer of a box of marrons glacés!' she avouches.

'I can confirm that as being true, my lord!' Erasmus says genially.

Lord Bortle stiffens.

'Miss Montez,' he says, 'kindly inform the other personage who is present that one does not wish to be addressed by him directly, since it reminds one of the regrettable fact of his continuing existence.'

'Trap shut, Erasmus!' Kitty snaps. Her tone changes as she returns her attention to the earl. 'Tell me, my lord, for I'm more than fascinated, if you find your beasts so unattractive, why do you continue to keep them? You might have spent your money in pursuit of wine, women and song.'

'Might one?' mutters Lord Bortle. 'Curse it, so one might! Oh well, too late to change now.' A far-off look steals across his features. 'The weaker creatures cower and cringe in the most gratifying manner when one whips them, and the stronger fawn over one when one deprives them of sustenance. One derives considerable pleasure from those sorts of things.'

Kitty leans in until she is conspiratorially close. 'It has been hinted to me by someone whose name I shan't mention that your lordship might possibly be interested in seeing the means by which your werewolf will be summoned.'

Lord Bortle sniffs.

'Curiosity is a vulgar trait, but one wouldn't object to a peek,' he says, feigning indifference.

Kitty brings out the amber ball from her reticule. The ball's surface is dull and still; its veins of fat appear as grey as stone.

'What the deuce is that?' asks Lord Bortle.

'A Siren Stone, my lord,' Kitty tells him. 'Used aright, it can rob any demon of its will, and turn it into a mindless slave.'

'I want it!' cries Lord Bortle. 'How much?'

'It is not for sale, my lord,' says Kitty.

Lord Bortle's face flushes crimson.

'What d'you mean, not for sale?' he roars. 'Everything in this man's world is for sale!'

Kitty weathers the earl's rage with a patient simper. 'Alas, my lord, the Siren Stone is not of this man's world. Besides, owning it would avail you nothing. In the hands of the uninitiated, the stone would be useless at best – at worst, a mortal danger.'

She gazes at Lord Bortle. Her eyes glow with an eldritch light. Within the light, the earl makes out twisted figures being goaded into capering grotesquely.

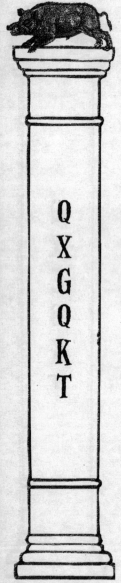

His nose detects a trace of sizzling torment.

Kitty blinks: the light is extinguished and the scent fades. She links arms with Lord Bortle and says, 'Did my lord mention tea earlier?'

'One did,' admits Lord Bortle. 'Tea, cakes, cucumber sandwiches, and so forth, and so on.'

Kitty and the earl set off towards Steyne House, with Erasmus scampering along behind them.

'Your lordship is fond of cucumber sandwiches?' enquires Kitty.

'One detests them!' Lord Bortle says with a shudder. 'But one has a duty . . . family tradition, and all that.'

Evening has descended on Wolveston, and all the lights of Broadway have been lit. In a backstage dressing room at the Egyptian Hall, Callisto, Crispin and Dessica await the evening performance. Crispin and Dessica are playing

Beggar-My-Neighbour. Both cheat, but Dessica cheats with greater aplomb.

Callisto is engrossed in the *Prattler*, the gossip column of the *Evening Hermes*. This acts as light relief after spending most of the afternoon with some of the more arcane tomes in his book collection, studying dragon lore.

To avoid prosecution for libel, the *Prattler* does not print in full the names of the individuals it mentions, but they are readily identifiable by those in the know. This evening's column is mostly unremarkable, until Callisto reads a passage that almost jolts him from his chair.

Can it really be that esteemed parliamentarian E*a*m*s S*i*e and wealthy nobleman L*r* B*r*t*e of S*e*n* H*u*e were engaged in an altercation at a certain Cambrian carvery on Broadway last night? The Prattler's sources are unshakeable in their conviction that the two gentlemen exchanged sharp words. Could their difference of opinion possibly be connected

Q
X
G
Q
K
T

with the alluring young woman who was dining at Mr S*i*e's table? Until now, the Prattler
has always considered that gentleman to be a
confirmed bachelor, but is that situation about
to change? Do we hear the distant chiming of
a matrimonial carillon? Has Eros's dart found
its mark, and in doing so, roused green-eyed
jealousy within an aristocratic bosom? Duelling
has long been outlawed in these Fair Isles, but it
is not unknown for two parties to travel to the
Continent in order to settle a Matter of Honour.
The Prattler awaits further developments with
the keenest of interest.

A passage from Captain Maroon's notebook seems to float before Callisto's eyes.

*With FM and ES to SH to meet LB.
Merciful Heaven, what a sink of
infernal depravity!*

ES is Erasmus Slike, Callisto thinks to
himself. LB is Lord Bortle, and SH must
be Steyne House. Lord Bortle is keeping a
collection of demons in the grounds of
his family home!

In her bedroom in Scarlatti Mews, Aril strains against the chains and straps that restrain her. Her bones are in flux; her face has become elastic and stretches itself into unnatural shapes; her teeth curve and sharpen; her fingernails turn black.

Mrs Moncrief tenderly mops sweat from Aril's brow, with a dampened napkin.

'There, there, Miss Aril!' she croons.

Aril can feel the rising moon pluck at her blood. She hears silver light being whispered against the rim of the horizon. A familiar dream leaps into being around her. She is at the edge of a jungle clearing, watching deer-like creatures as they graze. A wary stag flicks his ears and wags his tail.

Aril knows him, knows his scent, knows the sound his hooves will make on the jungle floor as he breaks into a run. A surge of power will drive her after him.

Branches will fly at her, like shadows. Her heart will pound, her tongue will loll . . .

The jungle sinks back down. The moon is up: tonight she is a dark-haired woman with a low, syrupy voice.

Come, Aril! the moon urges. *Come to me! Run to me!*

Aril groans.

Mrs Moncrief watches helplessly as coarse fur sprouts from her young mistress's skin. Aril's shoulders hunch, her waist narrows, her ears grow tall and pointed. She is more wolf than human now; the demon inside her is awake.

Chapter Thirteen:
A Nameless Destination

The audience has vacated the Egyptian Hall. The autograph hunters in Paradise Lane have been appeased, so Callisto, Crispin Rattle and Dessica Flaunt are free to make their way to the Embankment, where Callisto hails a rowing boat.

The ferryman heaves to. He has a weather-beaten face with white whiskers, and he is dressed in yellow oilskins and a sou'wester.

'Where to, squire?' he rasps.

'Three Rivals Wharf,' replies Callisto.

Caught between astonishment and alarm, the ferryman gapes. 'What d'you want to go there for?'

Dessica steps forward.

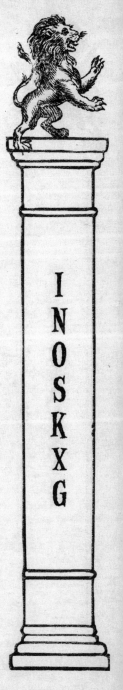

I N O S K X G

'None of your business, matey!' she says sharply. 'You going to take us there or not?'

The ferryman's fingernails rasp as he scratches his chin.

'Cost you three and a kick,' he essays.

Dessica snorts derisively.

'Don't you come it with me, matey!' she advises. 'The going rate's a florin, and you know it as well as I do.'

The ferryman curses under his breath and says, 'River girl, are you?'

'That ain't none of your business neither!' Dessica retorts. 'Quit nosing and get rowing.'

The ferryman helps his passengers aboard, then pulls on his oars under Dessica's critically watchful eye.

As the rowing boat progresses down-stream, the nature of the waterside changes. Grand memorials and sober government offices give way to buildings whose fabric has sagged into shabbiness. In once-proud lettering, a roofless warehouse with black-ened, burned-out windows proclaims itself, *FREE TRADE HOUSE.*

'Indigo Reach coming up on your right,' states the ferryman, apropos of nothing. 'My grandad worked there as a stevedore for thirty years. He reckoned that so many barges used to come up the Great Eastern Canal, you could walk across their decks to get from one side of the Bast to the other. Course, then some clever Dick went and invented the rail-ways. Broke the old man's heart when the docks shut down.' On the assumption that this anecdote has established a temporary intimacy between himself and his cus-tomers, the ferryman attempts to reason with Dessica. 'Are you sure about this trip? The Scarp ain't too healthy just now.'

'When's it ever been?' counters Dessica.

The ferryman can find no answer to this question, and is largely silent for the remainder of the journey.

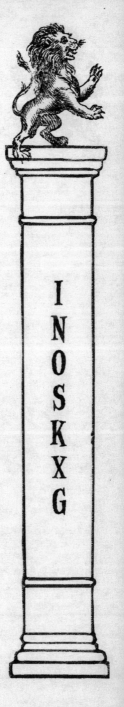

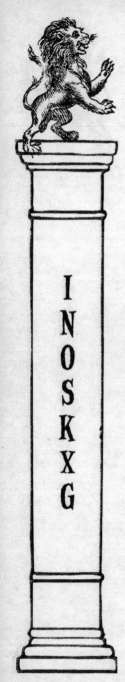

INOSKXG

* * *

Three Rivals Wharf is a wasteland where tumbledown sheds and storehouses huddle together as if for warmth. Water smacks and slaps against the quay. Iron bollards are collared with loops of rotted hawsers. Rusted coal-hoists loom like the skeletal remains of Titans. Nettles and brambles flourish in empty doorways.

Callisto selects a patch of concrete outside a brick shell that was formerly a marine chandler's premises. He opens the doctor's bag that he packed in Scarlatti Mews and took with him to the Egyptian Hall, brings out a corked bottle filled with what appears to be glittering sand, and hands it to Dessica.

'Pour that out in a big circle on the concrete,' he instructs her. 'Use it all, and don't get any in your eyes or mouth.'

'Why not?' says Dessica.

'If I told you that, you would be sorry

to have asked,' Callisto says grimly. 'Look lively!'

While Dessica is engaged in the circle's construction, Callisto takes Crispin aside, presses a purse of cash in his hand, and speaks to him furtively. 'If I don't return within twenty minutes of stepping into the circle, take Dessica back to Scarlatti Mews as quickly as you can, and use the money to get out of Wolveston with Aril and Mrs Moncrief – Dessica too, if she likes.'

'Where are you going?' Crispin enquires anxiously.

Callisto smiles. 'To a destination that doesn't have a name.'

'Can't I go with you?'

'I need you here, Crispin,' insists Callisto. 'I need to know that someone will look out for Aril and Dessica if the worst should happen. Can I rely on you to do that?'

Crispin nods; his eyes moisten.

'If it hadn't been for you, Mr Callisto, I

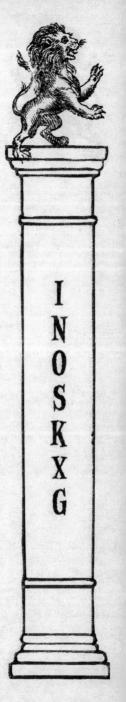

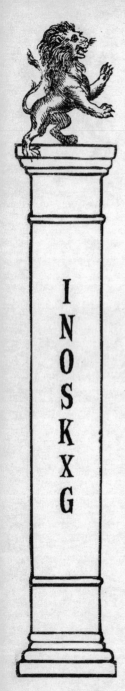

would have—!' He gulps. 'What I mean to say is—'

Callisto reaches out and gives the lad's shoulder a gentle squeeze.

'I know,' he says.

'Circle's done!' calls Dessica.

'Excellent, now stand well clear of it!' Callisto commands. 'Come what may, it's vitally important that you both stay outside the circle. Do you understand?'

'Yes!' chorus Crispin and Dessica.

Callisto draws a burnished copper disc from his bag. The disc is as large as a dinner plate, and is inscribed with symbols that are older than any human language. The magician steps over the line of glittering powder, stands in the centre of the circle, raises the disc to his face, and stares into it.

Crispin and Dessica watch, side by side.

'What's he—?' Dessica begins.

'Shh!' urges Crispin.

Where the notion comes from she

could not possibly say, but Dessica fancies that Callisto and the night are somehow intermingling. Darkness sifts into his solidity, dimming his outline so that it becomes indistinct.

And Callisto vanishes, leaving the copper disc hanging unsupported in the air.

'Where's he gone?' shouts Dessica.

She makes as if to run forwards, but Crispin holds her back.

'We mustn't go inside the circle!' he reminds her.

'But where'd he go?'

Because he cannot think of a comforting truth, Crispin settles for a valiant lie.

'Mr Callisto knows what he's doing,' he asserts. 'He'll be back in no time, don't you worry, Dess.'

Dessica treads heavily on Crispin's toes.

'Don't call me "Dess"!' she snaps.

Callisto is on a plateau, just below the jagged peak of a mountain. To his left,

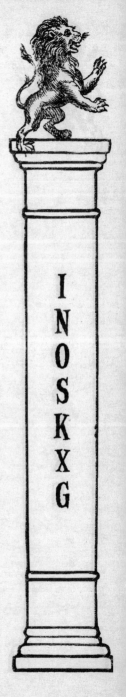

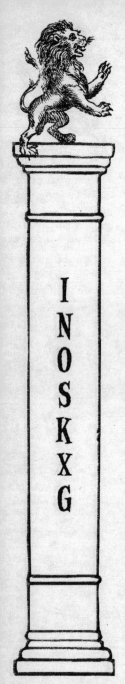

sheer cliffs of granite plunge into a narrow valley where a forest of firs grows in thick green billows. High above his head, in the blue depths of the sky, dragons sport, twisting and feathering like wisps of cloud. Their screeching cries sound faintly in Callisto's ears.

A movement causes him to turn.

The mountain opens a pair of enormous golden eyes. What Callisto took for a tortured crag is a colossal black she-dragon. The countless fathoms of her body are coiled tightly around the mountain top. Her claws are sunk in rock. Walled in behind scales and buttressed in bone, she is her own stronghold, an unassailable fortress.

The dragon speaks. At the sound of her voice the ground trembles, the air recoils, the heavens flinch.

'Who presumes upon my patience?'

'A humble human, Glorious One,' says Callisto.

The dragon vents two plumes of sulphurous smoke from her snout.

'You do not belong here, Earthborn!' she rumbles.

Callisto bows.

'Every second that I pass in your presence, the louder my heart clamours that this is so, Your Magnificence!' he exclaims. 'But I beg you to grant me a boon.'

The dragon laughs a roaring spout of fire into the sky. Her claws flex, and a curtain of pulverized stone drops in an avalanche.

'A boon?' she thunders. 'Who dares demand a boon of me?'

Callisto chooses his words with care, for his life depends upon them.

'I would not dare to demand anything of you, Lady of Dread,' he says, 'and though I am a fool, I am not so foolish as to give a dragon my name.'

The dragon shows her fangs in a grin.

'I suspect there may be a tiny germ of

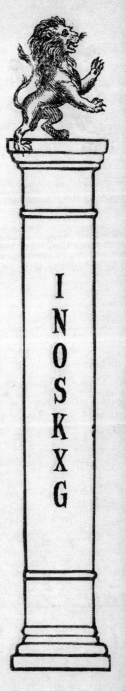

I
N
O
S
K
X
G

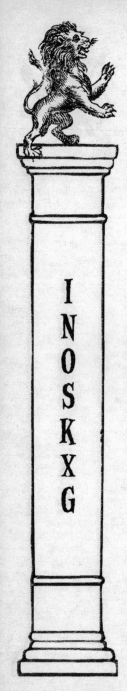

wisdom in you,' she allows. 'Tell me, are all humans as mildly diverting?'

'Your praise will be the solace of my dying moment, Lava Mother!' vows Callisto.

'A flattery too far, and you're an ember, human!' the dragon threatens. 'What is it that you want?'

'Nothing for myself,' reveals Callisto. 'One of your matchless brood was torn from this happy world by wicked members of my species. My only desire is the safe return of your offspring.'

'And you wish me to supply you with the means?' the dragon surmises.

Callisto spreads his hands. 'I am too puny to accomplish the task alone.'

'So I see!' the dragon drawls. 'Very well, I shall allow you what is required. Show your gratitude by never returning to my domain.'

She uncoils her tail; its tip flicks Callisto into darkness.

The darkness seethes and forms grains that fall like snow. Behind the grains stand Crispin and Dessica, Three Rivers Wharf, and the glare of Wolveston's lights in the night sky.

'Mr Callisto?' cries Crispin.

'I'm all right,' Callisto tells him. 'Stay where you are!'

He takes the copper disc from the air and places it at his feet, just as a wonder appears on the concrete in front of him, a pearl as big as a child's head, surrounded by an aura of white fire. The licking flames shoot out shadows across the desolate dockland.

A wave appears out on the Bast, and surges rapidly towards the wharf. The wave moves alongside the quay from left to right, then from right to left, as though it were conducting an inspection. With an abruptness that makes Crispin and Dessica gasp, a magnificent and monstrous head rears up. Claws clutch the

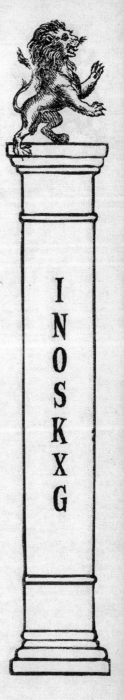

I
N
O
S
K
X
G

163

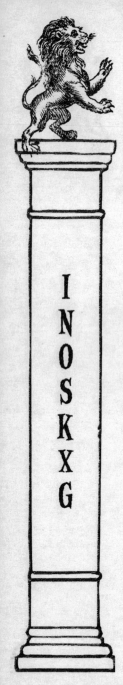

stone blocks at the quay's edge. A male dragon, golden-orange in colour, clambers out of the river.

He is the size of a cart horse, and Callisto estimates that he is less than a century old, hardly more than a toddler in human terms.

The dragon shakes a spray of water from his scales, and gazes longingly at the blazing pearl. His facial feelers lash and crack like whips, and he hisses happily, for at last in this soft, bland world, he has met with something familiar. He edges forward, then skulks back. The pearl tempts him, but he is unsure of the nearby humans.

'What's wrong with him?' Callisto mutters. 'Why won't he take the pearl?'

''Cos he's been bitten once, and now he's shy!' declares Dessica. She squats down, and clicks her fingers to attract the dragon's attention. 'Come on then!' she coos. 'Don't be scared, my handsome.'

The curious dragon cocks his head to one side.

'No one's going to hurt you,' says Dessica. 'You could rip us to bits easy, but wouldn't you rather have the pearl instead? Ain't it beautiful?'

The dragon recognizes a wistful tone in Dessica's voice: like him, she is an outsider. His caution collapses and he leaps upon the pearl. They whirl together in a vortex like the swaying column of air above the plughole of a draining bath. The pearl's flames flare until they are too bright to look at, and then there is nothing.

Dessica blinks away lilac after-images as Callisto steps out of the circle.

'You didn't kill him, did you?' she says.

'No,' says Callisto. 'I sent him home to Mum.'

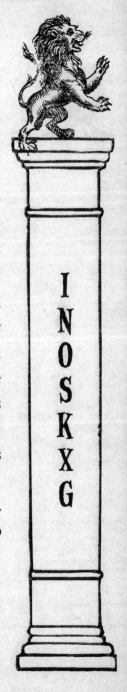

Chapter Fourteen:
Masters of Destiny

Lord Bortle has found Kitty Montez so diverting, and her offer to allow him to be present as she wields the Siren Stone so intriguing, that he puts aside his differences with Erasmus Slike, and issues an invitation for them to take pot luck with him at supper in Steyne House. Once this homely fourteen-course repast has been consumed, the earl and his guests retire to the relative intimacy of the Blue Drawing Room, which acts as the repository of Lord Bortle's hunting trophies. In his youth, Lord Bortle travelled the globe in pursuit of his passion for killing, and shot everything from aardvarks to zorillas. The stuffed heads of his prey, mounted on plaques and hung on the walls, stare down with sightless glass eyes as Puddifoot, the earl's Deputy Chief Underbutler-in-minor, draws the curtains, lowers the lamps, pours the liqueurs and sets out the humidors of fine cigars, before making so discreet an exit that afterwards no one can be entirely certain that he was ever present.

Lord Bortle invites Kitty and Erasmus to be seated around a circular marble-topped table, and is delighted when Kitty helps herself to a cigar, which she trims with a bite, and ignites with a mysterious wave of her left hand. She puffs out a series of smoke rings, which interlink and descend upon the heads of her besotted companions.

'Ah, Miss Montez!' sighs Lord Bortle. 'One does admire a woman who indulges her vices.'

'Then your admiration will know no bounds, my lord,' says Kitty, 'for I've

GLGTI

167

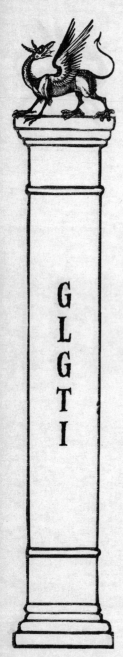

more vices than there are stars in the sky.'

Lord Bortle lights his own cigar with a Vesta.

'Tell me, Slike,' he says through a cloud of fragrant smoke, 'where did you find this captivating creature?'

'I didn't, my lord,' confesses Erasmus. 'As I recall, it was she who found me.'

'Lucky blighter!' Lord Bortle grunts.

'Not in the long run,' Kitty confides. 'Is your lordship ready for the demonstration?'

Lord Bortle nervously clears his throat.

'Is it like a séance?' he enquires. 'Should we join hands?'

Kitty regards Lord Bortle in the manner of a nanny catching one of her charges with his hand inside a biscuit barrel.

'It will be nothing like a séance, my lord,' she assures him. 'Séances are mere mummery, enacted by charlatans in order to fleece the gullible. What you are about to witness is an exhibition of genuine occult power. Whether or not you and Mr Slike feel inclined to hold hands is a matter you must decide for yourselves.'

Kitty produces the Siren Stone, places it on the table and whispers a few words in a language so inhumanly sharp that the drawing room window-panes buzz in their frames. The Siren Stone responds immediately: its opacity succeeds to an amber luminescence; the grey striations that riddle it quicken to a vivid white.

In the depths of the stone, Kitty espies the dragon that she dispatched to Wolveston earlier. The dragon's enthralment is complete enough for her to dispense with spoken words; her thoughts are sufficiently imperative.

'You can see the beast?' asks Lord Bortle.

'I can indeed, my lord,' Kitty affirms. 'It is making steady progress down the Bast and— oh!'

The scene within the stone wavers, and

G
L
G
T
I

169

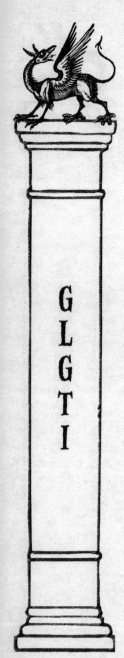

is replaced by a blankness that is filled with a prickling of pale dots.

'What is it, Treasure?' Erasmus says.

'Interference,' says Kitty primly. 'I shan't elaborate, for it would place too much of a strain on your limited intelligence.'

The blankness in the stone blinks, and an image reappears. The dragon is at Three Rivals Wharf, facing Callisto and the fiery pearl.

Kitty chuckles.

'Now that *is* resourceful!' she declares. 'I didn't foresee it.'

'Foresee what?' demands Lord Bortle.

The dragon pounces, merges with the pearl's white flames – and the Siren Stone falls dull and lifeless.

'I am afraid that your dragon is lost, my lord,' says Kitty.

'Don't talk nonsense!' the earl blusters. 'A dragon is far too big an animal to lose.'

'I fear that we have been stymied by an exceptionally gifted demonist who has returned the dragon to its own world,' says Kitty.

Lord Bortle is so distraught that he does not perceive the triumphant glint in Kitty's eyes.

'Lost and gone, lost and gone!' he keens. 'My lovely, lovely Draggy! I used to make it weep, you know. Its tears were as hot as cocoa.' He turns on Erasmus. 'What have you done, you bumbling fool?' he rages.

'I, my lord?' quails Erasmus. 'Why, I have done nothing!'

'Just so!' Lord Bortle fumes. 'You were content to sit back and let Miss Montez risk all, you spineless apology for a man! One has half a mind to fetch one's horse whip and—'

'My lord?' Kitty interrupts. 'The blame is entirely mine. I have employed a subterfuge. I used the dragon in order to distract the demonist from discovering our primary purpose.'

'The werewolf!' exclaims Lord Bortle.

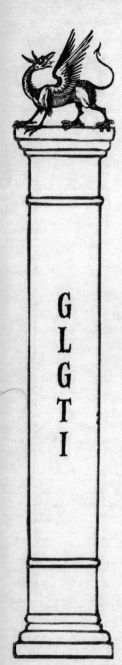

'Miss Montez, your deviousness renders one breathless. Am I to have my werewolf at last?'

Kitty smiles.

'I think I dare hazard to say that, before the night is out, you will have received everything that you deserve, my lord,' she purrs.

There are no cabs to be had in the Scarp after dark, so Callisto, Crispin and Dessica set out on foot along Dock Road.

'What was that copper thing, Mr Callisto?' Crispin says curiously.

'An ancient mirror that allowed me to find my way into another world,' replies Callisto. 'Few appreciate how singular an object a mirror is. When we look in one, we see things switched around, so that left is right, and right is left. A mirror shows us an alternative world to the one that we live in.'

'And what was that burning pearl about?' Crispin wonders.

'In paintings, Chinese dragons are frequently depicted toying with such jewels,' says Callisto. 'The pearl represents a spiritual perfection that naturally counterbalances the dragon's ferocity. Once the two have combined—'

Dessica stops walking, and cries, 'Frollies! Now I get it!'

'Get what?' says Callisto.

'You!' Dessica snaps. 'That wasn't no conjuring trick back there, was it? That was more than pulling a top hat out of a rabbit's ear, or sawing a lady into flags – that was real magic!'

Callisto pulls at his shirt collar, scratches his neck, and says, 'I have been known to dabble in the Dark Art, from time to time.'

Dessica narrows her eyes.

'What kind of bloke are you?' she says.

'The decent kind!' Crispin tells her. 'The

GLGTI

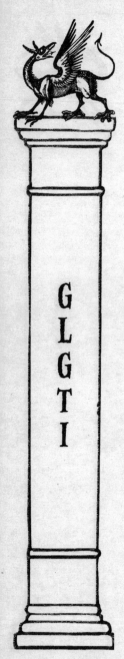

generous kind. The kind kind. Mr Callisto only uses magic to do good.'

'Whose good?' retorts Dessica. 'When you come right down to it, who's to say what's good and what ain't?'

'You are,' Callisto says, 'and until you make up your mind, you'll have to take me as you find me.'

'I ain't afraid of you, Callisto!' snarls Dessica.

'I don't require you to be afraid of me,' Callisto says. 'At present, all I require is that you go on walking. I'm anxious to get home and find out how Aril is.'

Dessica sheathes her defiance, for Aril is another matter entirely. She respects Aril, and the fact that Aril trusts Callisto would seem to suggest that he is trustworthy, magic notwithstanding.

Dessica shrugs and says, 'Let's get going then.'

Fortuitously, a cab is waiting on the corner of Bearwood Street, the westernmost border of the Scarp. The cab takes Callisto, Crispin and Dessica along Castle Road, past the Big Wheel and the crumbling remains of Wolveston Castle, then turns right onto Pym Way, where Callisto calls a halt at an all-night telegraph office, from which he sends a cable to Squalida MacHeath.

```
KILLER IS NO MORE - STOP
- MAINTAIN MAXIMUM VIGILANCE -
STOP - EXPECT ME EARLY
TOMORROW - STOP - C
```

As soon as he steps out of the cab in Scarlatti Mews, Callisto sees that something is wrong. A closed carriage is drawn up outside Number 17, and Mrs Moncrief has not lit the porch lamp, as is her wont. Callisto pays the driver and cautiously advances up the front path, with Crispin and Dessica lagging safely behind.

The front door is opened by a tall,

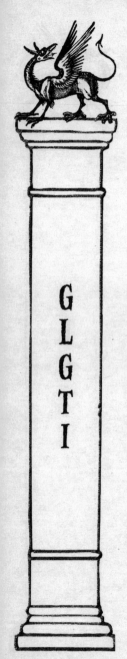

broad-shouldered man who wears a caped raincoat. Another raincoated man stands in the hall, with his hand resting on Mrs Moncrief's shoulder. The housekeeper's posture, with lowered head and shoulders, suggests abject shame.

'Mr Callisto?' says the man at the door.

Callisto senses authority, but his tone is nevertheless hostile as he says, 'Who are you, and what are you doing in my house?'

The man reaches inside his coat and brings out a leather wallet, which he flips open to reveal an enamelled badge. The badge shows a portcullis with a glaring eye at its centre. Beneath it is the inscription, *Quis custodiet ipsos custodes? – Who should guard the guard?*

It is the emblem of the Custodiate, the Lord Protector's Intelligence Service.

'I am Lieutenant Babcock, and my associate is Sergeant Zinzan,' says the man. 'Can you confirm that you instructed this woman, Mrs Letitia Moncrief, to consult the National Library's copy of the Army Register in order to obtain information about a certain captain in the First Wolveston Lancers?'

'I can give you a perfectly rational explanation for that,' Callisto says; then, remembering that a Chinese dragon is involved, he hastily adds, 'Well, an explanation at any rate.'

The lieutenant nods curtly.

'Sergeant Zinzan and I have no interest in any explanation, sir,' he says, 'but we are under orders to convey you to someone who is keenly interested.'

'You are taking me into custody?' proposes Callisto.

'I am requesting your cooperation, sir,' the lieutenant counters.

'As you wish,' says Callisto. 'If you and the sergeant would step outside and allow me a moment's privacy?'

With quiet firmness, the lieutenant says,

G
L
G
T
I

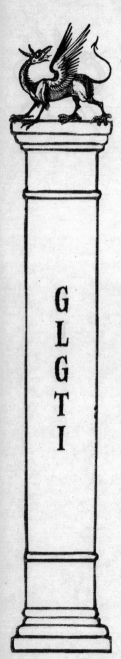

G
L
G
T
I

'I regret that won't be possible, sir.'

'Mr Callisto, I have failed you!' wails Mrs Moncrief. 'They questioned me and questioned me, until I didn't know which way round my head was on. I confessed everything!'

'Quite right too, Mrs M!' Callisto says. 'We've done nothing wrong, so there's nothing to fear.'

But despite his confident words, the magician is afraid. He is submitting himself to authority, to be sure, but to whose authority?

High above the Scarp, the moon is coy behind a cloud. People have taken to the streets: male and female, young and old alike. They are armed with whatever weapons came to their hands – daggers, cutlasses, pistols and rifles. A few carry antiquated flintlocks and blunderbusses. Those with cudgels rap them on walls and pavements as they go. Their faces are grim, their mouths are set. Tomcats howl and flee as the sparking hobnails of the crowd's boots approach.

United in a silent determination, people from all over the Scarp converge on Gospelmaker Road. They stream out of side streets and back alleys, their tributaries forming a high tide of bodies that surges towards St Augustine's.

The Scarp's inhabitants are done with cowering from a nameless, murderous enemy. They mean to make themselves masters of their own destiny, or die in the attempt.

Chapter Fifteen:
Night Manoeuvres

This is the Officer's Mess in Toolham Barracks, at nigh on midnight. Most of the personnel took to their beds long since, and the barracks has given itself up to darkness and snoring, but in the mess an oil lamp burns on a table where two uniformed men sit playing cards. They have been well supplied with a bottle of brandy, a soda-siphon, a tobacco pouch and three packets of cigarette papers. One of the card-players is Field Marshal Sir Jarvis Barkshaw, the other is Brigadier Plumpton Drury.

Sir Jarvis's spirit is still as greedy for self-indulgence and late hours as it ever was, but the fact is that his body has not been up to the mark for some while. His face is pale and drawn, his eyes are bloodshot. When he breathes, his lungs wheeze like a harmonium, as well they might, for he has been smoking incessantly for hours, and the fringes of his white moustache have been stained ginger with nicotine.

Brigadier Drury is younger, though old enough for his brown hair to be streaked with silver. His looks are somewhat marred by a sabre scar that pulls down the lower lid of his left eye, and continues across his cheek as far as his chin.

Sir Jarvis extinguishes the stub of a cigarette in an ashtray made from the case of a spent artillery shell.

'No news of Maroon, I suppose?' he says gruffly.

'None, sir,' says the brigadier. 'We haven't found any trace of him over the past few days, and it's the worst possible moment for him to go absent without leave. He's been pretty shaky these last

Z X U R R

Z X U R R

few weeks. It smacks of desertion to me.'

'Can't understand it!' Sir Jarvis mutters. 'Strapping young feller. Right-minded. Dashing and audacious. Whole life in front of him.'

'Audacity commonly leads to reckless-ness, sir,' pronounces the brigadier. 'Maroon was, as you know, a compulsive gambler, and deeply in debt.'

'Doxies and debt, downfall of many a young officer,' Sir Jarvis remarks. 'Not us though, eh, Plummy?'

He places a card on the table.

The brigadier plays a card, and wins a trick.

'We had the good taste to keep our indiscretions quiet, sir,' he says.

Sir Jarvis is in the mood to reminisce, and he basks in the comforting glow of past triumphs.

'Remember how we did for the Russkies at Sevastapol, Plummy?' he says.

'Yes, sir,' the brigadier responds with a

nod. 'We supplied them with grain, rice, bully beef, olive oil and medical equipment. The whole town would have starved without us.'

Sir Jarvis lifts a hand to conceal his blackened teeth as he yawns.

'We were glorious, Plummy!' he says. 'Bright-eyed, stout-armed, vim and vigour to spare. What happened?'

'Almost twenty-five years happened, sir, and we aged,' replies the brigadier. 'The world passed on to another generation.'

Sir Jarvis slaps his palm against the table.

'We'll win it back, Plummy!' he vows. 'Scarp purged, Parliament packed off, Lord Protector exiled, Queen Mariah enthroned. Heroes of the hour. Salad days restored. Young again, Plummy. Young!'

The brigadier is perturbed. Sir Jarvis has become all too liable to soundings-off in this vein, and on occasion, his pronouncements have come perilously close

Z
X
U
R
R

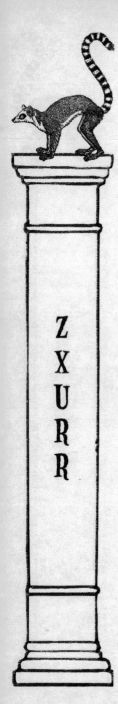

ZXURR

to senile ramblings. The brigadier has known the field marshal for most of his adult life and would, if need be, follow him into the maw of death – a spot to which, the brigadier has begun to suspect, they might both be doomed.

The brigadier laughs to cover his unease. 'If only rejuvenation were that simple, sir.'

Sir Jarvis seems surprised by his reaction. 'It is that simple, Plummy!' he insists. 'My belly's big, my whiskers are white – agreed! But don't be fooled. All put right in a trice. Trim waist, blood refreshed, spring in step, twinkle in eye.'

The brigadier feels icy teeth gnawing at the pit of his stomach as it dawns on him that his superior officer, the architect of Operation Osiris, is both serious, and seriously unhinged. He can think of absolutely nothing to say, and is relieved when his conversation with the field marshal is unexpectedly interrupted.

A signals officer enters the mess, marches smartly over to Sir Jarvis, and presents him with a folded paper and a crisp salute.

'From Wolveston, sir!' he brisks.

Sir Jarvis's hands tremble as he opens the paper and reads. His eyes bulge and his breathing grows heavier.

'Bad news, sir?' the brigadier ventures.

'No, good!' says Sir Jarvis. 'The best! Scarp's risen up. Operation Osiris is on.' He addresses the signals officer. 'Cable to Wolveston. We go in at dawn!'

In the Blue Drawing Room of Steyne House, Kitty Montez lowers her face to the Siren Stone, and rekindles its radiance by crooning an outlandish lullaby that sets the jets of the gaslights guttering.

'Daughter of the Moon!' she murmurs. 'Come to me, run to me!'

In her bedroom at Scarlatti Mews, Aril growls, for she can hear the murmuring

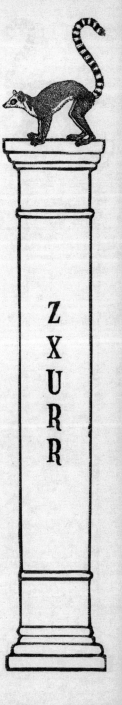

Z X U R R

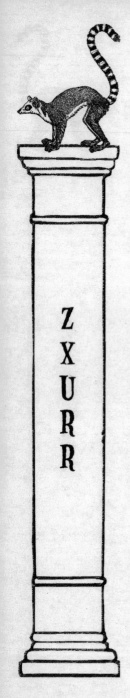

voice. She cannot catch the words, but the voice's tone stirs her memory, and carries her back to her desolate childhood, when she was an exhibit in a fair that toured the villages of the Indian subcontinent.

Aril was almost always in her wolf form then. If she chanced to wake up human, her owner would savage her with a malacca cane until she changed back. With dreadful clarity, she sees again the bars of the cage that was her prison, and the terrified expressions on the villagers who paid to gawp at her. Their fear quickly turned to contempt, and she hears their taunts and insults, feels once more the spiteful poking of their pointed sticks. Worst of all, Aril remembers how she believed that she deserved no better, and that it was her unalterable lot to be goaded and hurt.

And then she recalls the pale-faced, black-haired man with the crooked half smile, the man who looked into her cage and was not afraid; the man whose eyes filled with tears of pity when he saw what she had become, and who risked his life to set her free.

'Callisto!' she whines.

The voice sounds more clearly. 'He is in peril. Only you can save him. Hurry! Come to me, run to me!'

Crispin Rattle and Dessica Flaunt support a shaken Mrs Moncrief as she lurches into the kitchen, and lowers herself onto a chair. Aware of the faith the housekeeper has in the restorative powers of liquorice water, Crispin locates a bottle in the pantry, and Mrs Moncrief doses herself with a goodly swig.

'A thousand thanks for your thoughtfulness, Master Crispin!' she sighs. 'I thought I was a goner for sure.'

'It'll take more than a couple of Custodiate agents to finish you off, Mrs

Z
X
U
R
R

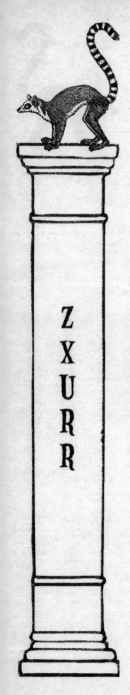

Z
X
U
R
R

M!' Crispin says cheerily. 'Tough as old boots, you are!'

Mrs Moncrief fixes him with a querulous eye.

'Old, but still fashionable boots of kid leather!' Crispin jabbers. 'Hardly any wear on them at all! Not even old, really!'

'Never mind all that malarkey, what about Callisto?' cries Dessica. 'Where have they taken him, and how are we going to spring him?'

'Those who are in the custody of the Custodiate cannot be sprung, Miss Flaunt,' states Mrs Moncrief. 'They are either returned to liberty, or are never heard of again.'

Dessica shuffles her feet in an ecstasy of restlessness.

'The Custodiate spy on people, don't they?' she says.

'Spies are employed by foreign powers,' Mrs Moncrief corrects her. 'The agents of the Custodiate are the guardians of our liberty.'

'But what are we going to *do*?' groans Dessica. 'We can't just sit here.'

Mrs Moncrief ponders, then says, 'A game of draughts can be most soothing – or a mug of malted milk perhaps?'

An expletive of startling profanity rises to Dessica's lips, but before she can deliver it, Crispin speaks up.

'Mr Callisto would want us to stay put and look after Aril,' he says. 'When she's fit to travel, we should get out of Wolveston. Mr Callisto gave me some money to tide us over.'

'And where, pray, would we go?' says Mrs Moncrief.

'I've been giving that some thought, and I reckon London would be best,' Crispin tells her. 'No one would think of looking for us there. No one would think of looking for *anybody* in London.'

Dessica is impressed. There is a calm

Z
X
U
R
R

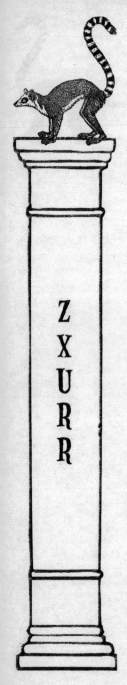

Z X U R R

authority about Crispin that she has not seen before.

'How d'you know someone's going to look for us?' she enquires.

'Because this is all about the government, and the army, and secrets, and the League of the Golden Unicorn,' says Crispin. 'We know most of what Mr Callisto knows, and the Custodiate have already been for him. We could be next.'

This makes perfect sense to Dessica, although she wishes that it did not.

'You were talking about Aril being fit to travel,' she says. 'Is she ill or something?'

An invisible defensive wall descends in the kitchen. Crispin and Mrs Moncrief are on one side of the wall, while Dessica is on the other.

'It's, well, u-u-m . . .' says Crispin.

Mrs Moncrief waffles. 'It is a matter of considerable delicacy. Naturally, given her tender years and sensibilities, Miss Aril is somewhat sensitive. It wouldn't do for

Master Crispin or myself to discuss her private affairs with – I hope you will forgive me for saying so, Miss Flaunt – a relative stranger. However, I'm certain that as you become better acquainted with her, Miss Aril will—'

There is a tremendous thrashing and crashing upstairs. Metal squeals and pings; rivets pop, wood splinters, glass shatters. From outside comes a warbling howl that would clot single cream.

'Aril!' shouts Crispin.

He almost collides with Mrs Moncrief as they both rush for the kitchen door. Mrs Moncrief lets Crispin through, then follows him upstairs, with Dessica close behind.

Aril's room is in disarray. Her broken bed has been overturned, the chains and straps that bound her have been snapped as if they were strips of toffee. The window is a gaping, jagged gap in the wall.

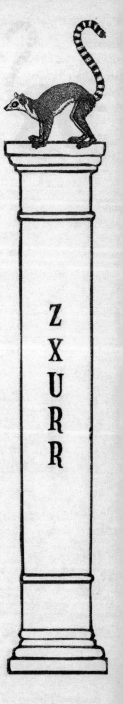

Z X U R R

Z X U R R

Accurately, if needlessly, Mrs Moncrief declares, 'Miss Aril . . . has gone!'

'We have to find her fast, before she hurts herself, or someone else!' exclaims Crispin.

Dessica is confused.

'What you talking about?' she says. 'Aril wouldn't hurt no one, would she?'

Crispin looks directly into Dessica's eyes, and speaks distinctly, so there will be no mistaking his words.

'Aril is a werewolf,' he says.

Chapter Sixteen:
The Man on Constitution Row

A multitude of thoughts races through Dessica Flaunt's mind as she matches the truth of what she has just learned about Aril against her personal impressions. What she took for regal aloofness was, in fact, restraint, and the atmosphere of mystery surrounding Aril was generated by an actual mystery, which has now been revealed.

'Aril, a werewolf?' Dessica snorts. 'Hmm, makes sense.'

Crispin frowns questioningly. 'You're not scared?'

'Not really,' Dessica says.

'Put off?'

'No.'

'Surprised?'

Dessica laughs.

'I'm from the Scarp, matey!' she says. 'Nothing surprises me. Which way did Aril go?'

'She might have gone in any direction!' frets Mrs Moncrief. 'In lupine mode, Miss Aril can trot at between eight and ten miles per hour, a speed which she can maintain indefinitely. For shorter periods, she can accelerate to thirty miles per hour.'

'Crumbs! Who's swallowed the encyclopedia?' Dessica teases.

Mrs Moncrief blinks coolly.

'I would strongly advise anyone who intends to keep house for a werewolf to research the topic thoroughly,' she says. 'The investment in time will yield a handsome dividend.'

'We haven't got any time *to* invest!' groans Crispin as he peers anxiously through the ruined window. 'She's getting further away every second.'

'We could do with a clue,' Dessica reasons.

'Or a stroke of good fortune,' adds Mrs Moncrief.

And at that very moment, both are granted simultaneously, for the moon casts off a wrap of cloud, and lights up Callisto's tiny but trim back garden.

'What's that?' says Dessica, pointing.

A line of phosphorescent drops runs the length of the garden. Each drop glows a greenish-yellow, like the shine in the back of a cat's eyes.

'Look here!' Mrs Moncrief exclaims.

A splash of dark liquid is glowing on the window-sill.

'Miss Aril must have sustained a cut when she hurled herself headlong through the casement,' Mrs Moncrief deduces. 'Moonlight renders her blood luminous. All we have to do is follow the trail.'

'If Aril goes as fast as you say, we don't

stand no chance of catching her up on foot,' Dessica points out.

Mrs Moncrief holds her head high.

'Then we shall not proceed on foot!' she announces grandly. 'Master Crispin, Miss Flaunt, allow me to collect my bonnet and my umbrella, and we are away!'

Mrs Moncrief strides along Pinchbeck Street with Crispin and Dessica in her wake. She turns left into Caraway Alley, a cul-de-sac that ends in a pair of stout wooden doors which have been lettered thus:

Amos Toper
Livery Stables & Cab Hire
Equine Accommodation
for the Discerning
Conveyances for the Connoisseur

The doughty housekeeper grasps the ferrule of her umbrella, uses its goose-head handle to beat out a lively tattoo on the doors and, in a bellow like a bull-moose in the mating season, calls out, 'Open up!'

Before long, a voice is heard grumbling on the other side of the doors. 'All right, all right! I was fast asleep until you started up your racket.'

'Commerce never sleeps, Amos Toper!' retorts Mrs Moncrief. 'Here's business waiting to be done.'

Locks snicker, chains chink, bolts rattle. One of the doors swings back to reveal a man in a flannel night-shirt and a tasselled night-cap. He holds a lantern in his left hand, and the lantern's light spills over his round face. His curly grey hair resembles a sheep's fleece. The delight in his eyes is magnified by the lenses of his rimless spectacles.

'Letitia!' he cries. 'Can it be you?'

J
X
G
M
U
T

'It can be, and it is,' says Mrs Moncrief. 'I apologize for the inconvenience of the hour, but I am in urgent need of a cab.'

Amos Toper throws the door open wide.

'You could never be an inconvenience to me, Letitia!' he says. 'The choice of cab is yours.'

He is so clearly smitten with Mrs Moncrief that Crispin and Dessica look at each other with raised eyebrows.

Then a thought occurs to Dessica.

'Who's going to drive this here cab?' she asks.

'Mrs M,' says Crispin. 'She's a fully qualified cabbie.'

'Licence number 14287,' Mrs Moncrief states proudly. 'Cab driving is an accomplishment which has come in handy more often than you might suppose.'

In a matter of minutes the cab horses are rigged and ready, and Mrs Moncrief, Crispin and Dessica embark upon their quest.

Dessica's night-vision, honed by years of vigilance on the Bast, proves to be an invaluable asset. She quickly sights Aril's shining spoor in nearby Eden Street. The trail leads to Barebones Throughway, which runs parallel to the Western Railway that links Wolveston to the prosperous townships of North Wales. The through-way is long and straight, and was built for speed. Mrs Moncrief urges the cab horses to a canter.

Dessica has her head out of the cab window, and as the vehicle's increased velocity causes her hair to stream out behind her head, she laughs aloud, and proclaims, 'This is better than plum duff!'

In another cab, in another district of the city, Callisto is being transported to he knows not where. Despite the presences of Lieutenant Babcock and Sergeant Zinzan, the journey is silent, for agents of

199

the Custodiate have no small talk, and precious little large talk either.

Callisto considers his options. He could effect an escape without difficulty. By employing his persuasive mesmeric powers, he could entrance his companions, pick the locked door of the cab, and dive out into the night.

But would escape bring me any advantage, he wonders to himself, or would I just be jumping from a leaky lifeboat into a shark-infested sea? And is this the lifeboat or the ocean?

He listens carefully to every noise that comes from outside. They must have entered a busy part of Wolveston, for the cab proceeds slowly, and Callisto hears passing traffic and a muffled hubbub of voices. Only Broadway would be so populous so late.

The cab executes a turn into a quieter thoroughfare, and then a second turn. The clatter of the horses' hooves, which has echoed brightly from surrounding buildings, takes on the duller tone of the open air.

The cab stops. The driver gets down and opens the door.

'Step outside, Mr Callisto,' instructs Lieutenant Babcock.

Castillo knows at once where he is – on Constitution Row, in Parliament Park. Below him, at the foot of a gentle incline, the Parliament Building, ablaze with lights, twinkles like a palace carved from crystal.

A voice to Callisto's right says, 'A fine sight, is it not? I never tire of it.'

Callisto turns and sees the best-known face in Greater Britain, the face whose profile adorns every coin about his person: the face of Lord Protector Groves.

The Lord Protector wears a long overcoat and a tall stovepipe hat. His cheeks are deeply lined. He wears his black whiskers

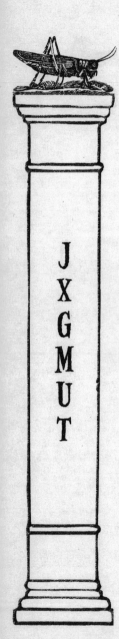

J X G M U T

in a beard, but his top lip is clean shaven. His nose is long and bony; his brown eyes are tired, and wise, and kind and sorrowful.

'Forgive the business with the closed cab, Callisto,' he pleads. 'Even I must follow the rules at times. It must be two years since we last met.'

'Three, Mr Groves,' says Callisto, employing the form of address that the Lord Protector prefers.

'Ah yes!' Mr Groves concurs. 'I seem to recall a tricky situation involving an Italian mystic and a tsarina.'

'A matter so trifling that I'm amazed you remember it,' remarks Callisto.

'Come, come, Callisto, no false modesty!' Mr Groves gently scolds. 'I still don't understand how you managed to resolve the problem without attracting the attention of the Press.'

'Magic,' Callisto says offhandedly.

Mr Groves's demeanour becomes serious.

'And now you've dished the dragon in the Scarp by the same means,' he says. 'I'm not sure whether that merits praise or admonition.'

Callisto is dumbfounded.

'You knew about the dragon?' he gasps.

Mr Groves nods solemnly. 'Lord Bortle evidently keeps quite a collection at Steyne House,' he says. 'And since I know about Lord Bortle, it follows that I also know about Erasmus Slike, Field Marshal Barkshaw and the League of the Golden Unicorn.'

Callisto's wonderment is allayed by a flash of anger.

'You knew about the plot to restore the monarchy, yet you did nothing to prevent the murders in the Scarp?' he snaps.

The hurt in the Lord Protector's gaze is almost palpable.

'You're free to criticize my decisions, Callisto, but bear in mind that you don't have to live with my conscience. The

J
X
G
M
U
T

future of the nation was at stake. I needed to know exactly who was involved, and the longer I let things alone, the more the Custodiate was able to discover about the extent of the conspiracy. I couldn't simply scorch the snake, I had to burn out its black heart. If I could have thwarted the treason and avoided the deaths in the Scarp, I would have done so. I did not take my decisions lightly.'

The cost is in the man's expression, and his air of weariness; he is fifty-six years old, but might easily be taken for twenty years older.

'Forgive my outburst, Mr Groves,' apologizes Callisto. 'I spoke too hastily.'

'You said nothing that I have not said to myself,' Mr Groves assures him. 'Matters are now in hand. Squalida MacHeath has been warned what to expect. Only one piece of the puzzle remains unplaced. Tell me, Callisto, have you heard of a young woman named Kitty Montez?'

'No,' says Callisto.

'She keeps company with Erasmus Slike,' continues Mr Groves, 'and I have strong reason to believe that she controlled the dragon with some sort of incandescent rock.'

'A Siren Stone?' Callisto marvels. 'But that's impossible! A human couldn't use it. Only a demon is capable of—' His jaws clamp shut. Between clenched teeth he hisses, 'Bazimaal!'

'You have lost me,' confesses Mr Groves. 'But listen, Callisto, I have it on the most reliable authority that Kitty Montez and Erasmus Slike are staying at Steyne House tonight. Furthermore, even as I speak they are attempting to kidnap your ward by utilizing the power of the stone. I regret to say that their attempt has so far been successful. Go to Steyne House with all possible dispatch, rescue your ward, and dispose of Lord Bortle's monstrous collection by any means you

consider expedient. However, let us be clear that in no way can I be seen to have any involvement in this. It cannot even be known that I know.' Mr Groves turns aside and says, 'Lieutenant Babcock?'

The lieutenant steps promptly from the cab. 'Sir?'

'Kindly escort Callisto to the headquarters of the Traction Squad,' says Mr Groves. 'An engine is standing by.'

Chapter Seventeen:
On the Trail

The headquarters of Wolveston Civic Constabulary's Traction Squad – or 'the Flying Boys' as they are popularly known – is to be found north of Parliament Square, in Naseby Yard, just off Wildman Street. The squad owes its existence to the mechanical ingenuity of Zachariah Bird, a pupil-turned-rival of Daniel Taft. Bird's invention of the asymmetrical bifurcated piston allowed steam engines to be considerably reduced in size, which led to the development of a new and powerful type of traction engine, capable of speeds in excess of thirty-five miles per hour. Only an express train offers a faster mode of transport.

As Callisto and Lieutenant Babcock disembark from the closed carriage, they see a traction engine waiting in the centre of the yard. It is all brass and copper tubing, cast-iron flywheels and thick tracks of reinforced rubber. The boiler has been painted bright green, the inverted cone of the funnel is black, with a red band around its rim. Fixed to the front of the boiler is a brass plate, inscribed with a rearing winged horse, and the motto: CELERITAS ET VERITAS – Speed and Truth.

A man crosses the yard, rubbing his hands with a filthy rag. He is short in stature and rotund of girth. His nose is big, his cheeks are fleshy and he has the mischievous grin of an impudent schoolboy. He wears a pair of navy-blue dungarees, and a remarkable flat cap. The cap has, variously, been worn, torn, tattered and battered, flayed, frayed, drenched in oil, dipped in grease and spotted with tar, and it resembles only itself, for nothing else in the world is like it.

'Mr Callisto,' says Lieutenant Babcock, 'allow me to introduce Leading Steersman Popplewell.'

'How do,' says the steersman. 'I won't shake hands, on account of I'm right mucky. I've just had to lubricate my reciprocators.'

'I'm pleased to make your acquaintance, Leading Steersman,' says Callisto.

The steersman rolls his eyes.

'Now then, none of that!' he says. 'The name's Hercules. Come and meet the engine. She's a Mark Seven Neptune Class, but I call her Dotty. You've probably noticed the chamfered edging on the inlet manifold – an interesting variation from standard is that . . .'

Hercules is a traction engine enthusiast, and like most enthusiasts, he assumes that everyone else is fascinated by the min-utiae of his particular area of expertise.

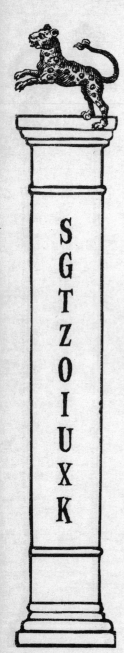

He reels off facts about gear ratios and boiler pressure with an energy which seems to hint that, deep inside, he has a little traction engine driving him.

Callisto interrupts an account of the relative merits of reaming and counter-sinking to ask, 'Who's that up in the cab?'

He is referring to a dungareed man who holds a shovel. The man is stick-thin and mournful of aspect. His eyes, shoulders and moustache droop to the same extent, and he seems permanently on the brink of tears.

'That's my stoker, Charlie Chiddock,' says Hercules. 'How's tricks, Charlie?'

'Never better,' Charlie says, without enthusiasm.

Hercules raises his cap and pops the filthy rag under it.

'But here's me rattling on about Dotty, when you've places to go!' he exclaims. 'Where d'you want taking?'

'Steyne House.'

'Never been there, but we'll look it up on the revolving gazetteer,' says Hercules. 'Climb aboard, and let's get gone.'

There is just room for three in the cab. Charlie shovels; Hercules taps dials, spins wheels and tugs at a lanyard.

The engine's whistle toots, the funnel chuffs, the tracks revolve. Slowly but smoothly, Dotty glides out of Naseby Yard, into Wildman Street.

The atmosphere in the Blue Drawing Room at Steyne House has turned decidedly uncomfortable. Erasmus Slike would be perfectly content to watch Kitty Montez whisper to the Siren Stone until he wasted away. Lord Bortle, on the other hand, has grown fidgety. He sucks his teeth and twiddles his thumbs; he lights a cigar he does not want, takes two puffs, mashes it out in a solid silver ashtray, and lights another.

'One is bored!' he announces petulantly. 'Bored, d'you hear? Bored, bored, bored!'

'I'm almost done,' Kitty informs him.

This does not satisfy the earl.

'One is still bored!' he grumbles. 'One thinks one might slip out to the Fabulary Garden and make something squirm. There's nothing so diverting as the suffering of dumb creatures, don't you find, Miss Montez?'

'Indeed I do, my lord,' Kitty replies satirically, 'though I fancy we might disagree as to what constitutes a dumb creature.'

There is a sound from the other side of the French windows, a scraping of nails on slabs of paving.

'Ah!' says Kitty. 'That must be the visitor we have been expecting.'

She stands up, crosses the room and draws aside a curtain.

Aril is standing on the terrace outside, still dressed in her white night-gown. The garment is besmirched and bespattered, and the torn hem hangs loose at one side.

Burrs and seeds have caught in her facial fur. Her yellow eyes seem dazed, and her wet black nose wrinkles as she sniffs, searching for a familiar scent. The crest of hair on her scalp alternately bristles and lies flat. She is tired, and thirsty, and confused, and her will has been sapped.

Erasmus shrieks.

Lord Bortle's face is livid.

'Great Mithras!' he croaks. 'It's hideous! Utterly hideous!'

Erasmus's initial terror subsides into mere shock.

'What's wrong with its, er, hand, or paw, or what you m'call it?' he quavers.

'Utterly hideous!' rasps Lord Bortle. 'Utterly, utterly hideous!'

'She is injured,' Kitty says to Erasmus. 'I'll let her in so we can dress the wound.'

Erasmus leaps to his feet, and sidles back towards the door.

'Kitty,' he says in a strained voice, 'are you quite certain that allowing it ingress

S
G
T
Z
O
I
U
X
K

would be entirely prudent? Limited as my experience of such matters is, I have gathered that the werewolf's temperament tends towards the homicidal.'

'Stop calling her "it", Erasmus!' snaps Kitty. 'She isn't a thing.'

'Utterly, utterly hideous!' Lord Bortle mumbles.

'Stop saying that!' Kitty rails. 'She is a beautiful werewolf. If you weren't so bigoted, you would see that for yourself.'

'Bigoted?' the earl says vaguely.

'Unreasonably intolerant and irredeemably prejudiced,' explains Kitty.

Lord Bortle nods.

'Quite right, m'dear!' he says. 'That's one down to a T.'

Kitty opens the French windows and speaks to Aril. 'You hear my voice and no one else's. You will do as I say, and only as I say. You will be whatever I instruct you to be.'

Aril whimpers like a distressed puppy.

* * *

While Callisto is setting off from Naseby Yard, Mrs Moncrief is inching the cab down a winding country lane so narrow that the branches of the hedgerows lining the way scrape against the vehicle's sides. She opens the little communications hatch in the roof of the cab, and calls, 'Any sign?'

'None,' comes the reply.

The search party's luck seems to have run out. They lost sight of Aril's trail shortly after leaving the Barebones Throughway, and are now searching somewhat aimlessly, in hopes of picking it up again.

Inside the cab, Crispin Rattle heaves the heaviest of sighs.

'She must have gone across the fields,' he says. 'We won't catch her now.'

'Does she often go off like this?' asks Dessica.

'No,' Crispin says. 'As far as I know, this

215

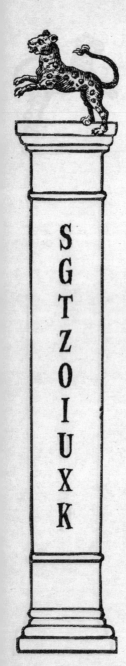

is the first time. Something must have got her monkey up good and proper.'

'How long have you known her?' says Dessica.

'A bit more than a year.'

Dessica hesitates a moment, then says, 'You sweet on her?'

'No!' Crispin asserts, as his face turns red.

'That blush of yours says different,' observes Dessica, with acuity. 'Don't you mind that she's a werewolf?'

Crispin's blush deepens. His feelings for Aril are complex; he has never discussed them with anybody before, and now he discovers that he does not much like doing so.

'She's still Aril when she's the werewolf,' he says, reasoning it out as he goes, 'and she's still the werewolf when she's Aril. If she wasn't like that, she wouldn't be who she is.'

Once more, Dessica feels a twinge of

regret, for she has no one in her life to care for what she is like, or to know who she is.

'You're lucky to have Aril, Callisto and Mrs Moncrief,' she says wistfully.

'And don't I know it!' says Crispin.

The lane suddenly joins a road. Directly opposite the junction stands a monumental arch, set into a high wall. The arch frames a pair of ornate wrought-iron gates. Affixed to one of the gates is a sign that reads:

STEYNE HOUSE
PRIVATE PROPERTY
KEEP OUT!

ADMISSION BY INVITATION ONLY
TRESPASSERS WILL BE MAULED!

'Stop a tick, Mrs M!' shouts Crispin, for he has espied a man keeping watch in a kiosk in the left-hand column of the arch. When the cab halts, Crispin steps out and crosses the road.

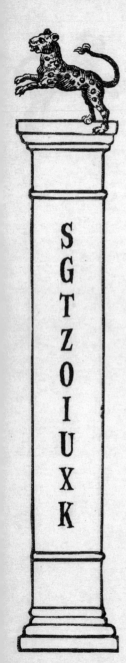

'Watcher, mate!' he greets the gate-keeper. 'You wouldn't happen to have seen a big funny-looking dog running round on its hind legs, would you?'

The gatekeeper looks the lad up and down, and spits at his feet.

'Sling yer hook!' he growls.

'All right, all right! Keep your shirt in!' says Crispin. He returns to the cab and, as he clambers in, remarks, 'Friendly lot round here, Mrs M. They'd slit your throat as soon as look at you.'

Mrs Moncrief turns the cab to the right. The wall goes on and on like a boring schoolteacher. It is topped with a row of viciously sharp iron spikes.

'Whoever owns that lot must be rolling in it!' comments Crispin. 'Doesn't want anyone getting in though.'

'Doesn't want anyone getting out neither,' Dessica jests, and then she frowns, for her memory has been jogged.

Before she is able to place the recollection, Crispin cries, 'Stop, Mrs M! Look over there!'

Dessica's gaze follows the direction of Crispin's pointing finger.

Glowing faintly in the light of the moon, a line of Aril's blood crosses the road and runs straight towards the wall.

Crispin, Dessica and Mrs Moncrief alight from the cab and conduct a hurried investigation.

There are traces of blood in the meadow opposite the wall, but no blood going to left or right at its foot.

'She couldn't have run straight through the wall, could she?' says Dessica.

Mrs Moncrief taps her umbrella on the road.

'It's my opinion that she jumped over,' she declares.

'What?' boggles Dessica.

'Mrs M's right,' Crispin assures her. 'When Aril's a werewolf, her strength is prodigious. She could hop this wall easy.'

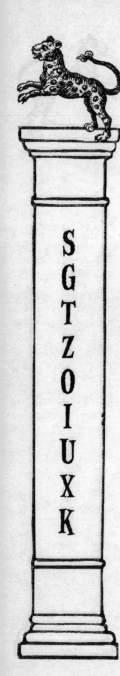

He glances upwards and rubs his hands together. 'Right!'

'Right what?' hoots Dessica.

'I'm going to climb up and drop down on the other side,' Crispin says.

Dessica laughs.

'Don't talk noggo!' she scoffs. 'That wall's twenty foot high and smoother than a baby's bum.'

'But all is not lost!' proclaims Mrs Moncrief. 'Cover your eyes, Master Crispin.'

Crispin does as he is bid and, in his self-imposed darkness, hears a tremendous rustling and bustling, and a gasp of wonder from Dessica, who says, 'Crispin? Cast your peepers on this lot!'

Crispin uncovers his eyes.

Laid out on the ground at Mrs Moncrief's feet are a coil of rope, a small grappling-hook and a policeman's truncheon.

'What's this?' says Crispin in bewilderment.

The resourceful housekeeper smiles.

'Since entering Mr Callisto's employ, I have become accustomed to expecting the unexpected,' she reveals. 'Therefore I make a point of never leaving the house without a few useful necessities.'

Crispin scratches the back of his head. 'Where d'you carry them, Mrs M?'

Mrs Moncrief tilts back her head, squints down her nose, and magnificently says, 'In my unmentionables!'

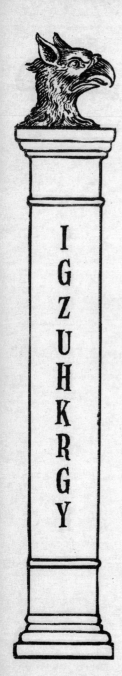

I G Z U H K R G Y

Chapter Eighteen:
Impasse

Dotty puffs and tickers down the Barebones Throughway. The beam of her headlamp probes the dark. Miniature comets and meteorites of sparks fly out with the smoke from her funnel.

Charlie Chiddock has fallen into an easy rhythm of work, and plies his shovel with grace and gusto.

Hercules Popplewell makes subtle adjustments to the steering, and sounds the whistle to warn slower traffic of Dotty's approach.

Callisto stares straight ahead through the driving cab's porthole, his face shining in the light from the flames in the fire-box. His outward stillness belies an inner turmoil. He cares as deeply for Aril as if she were his own daughter, and the idea of her being in the clutches of the hated demon Bazimaal fills him with apprehension. Bazimaal and Callisto have encountered each other more than once over the years, but the demon has always managed to avoid a confrontation to decide whose occult powers are the stronger. Tonight, Callisto is determined to have it out at last. If Bazimaal has done Aril the slightest harm, Callisto means to destroy the demon so thoroughly that not an atom of it will remain.

In the meantime, outside Steyne House, Mrs Moncrief has, with consummate skill, tossed up the grappling-hook and secured it between two of the iron spikes on top of the wall.

'Right, Mrs M,' Crispin says briskly, 'give me an hour, and if I haven't turned up by then, nip back to Wolveston, wait for Mr

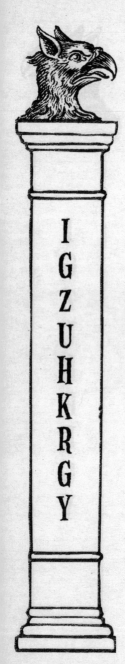

Callisto and tell him what's happened.' He gapes at Dessica, who has grasped the scaling rope in both hands. 'What d'you think you're doing?'

'Going first,' answers Dessica.

'No you're not!' Crispin protests. 'You're staying with Mrs M. This could be dangerous.'

Dessica pantomimes a terrified expression.

'Ooh, I'd better stick here and get on with my embroidery!' she mocks. 'Passed a law that says girls ain't allowed to be brave, have they?'

'No,' concedes Crispin, 'but I promised Mr Callisto that I'd look after you.'

Dessica regards him disdainfully.

'I can take care of myself, matey!' she snaps. 'What's the plan?'

Crispin sees that Dessica will brook no arguments, and since time is wasting, he surrenders.

'Go in, find Aril, and get out,' he says.

'Bit skimpy on details, ain't it?' observes Dessica. 'We don't even know for sure that she's in there, do we?'

'I feel it in my water,' Crispin maintains.

Dessica is not anxious for further elucidation. With the nimbleness of a rat scampering up a ship's hawser, she climbs the rope and balances herself between the rows of spikes. Crispin is quick to join her. They haul in the rope, alter the position of the grappling-hook and lower themselves into the grounds of Steyne House. After some initial casting about, Dessica detects a drop of Aril's blood on a rhododendron leaf, and they follow the trail onto a track that runs between a grove of horse chestnut trees.

'I don't like this, it's too quiet,' mutters Dessica. 'Toffs got man-traps, guard dogs, and night-watchmen. This is too easy.'

'Is that such a bad thing?' Crispin enquires.

'It's not right,' says Dessica. 'Something funny's going on.'

And then the goings-on become even funnier, for as Crispin and Dessica leave the cover of the trees, they see a male unicorn standing in a paddock directly in front of them. The unicorn is about the size of a Shetland pony, though of a considerably more elegant shape. His coat is dazzlingly white in the moonlight, his whorled horn is gunmetal blue, and he is unquestionably the most beautiful animal that Dessica has ever laid eyes on. She squeals in delight and, with no thought for her own safety, darts forward.

'Hang on!' urges Crispin, but he is too late.

Dessica clambers onto the gate of the paddock, and the unicorn ambles over to her. He gently presses the side of his head against her, and in his whinny Dessica hears an infinity of solitary sadness. She strokes his neck and mane, even though

226

she knows that she cannot give the beast sufficient comfort.

Crispin ventures closer, at which the unicorn abruptly shies away from Dessica, and retreats.

'You frightened him!' Dessica upbraids Crispin.

'I didn't mean to,' Crispin apologizes. 'What are those marks on his back legs?'

Dessica peers, and catches her breath.

'He's been whipped!' she says, seething. 'Someone's going to pay for that!'

Crispin and Dessica continue to follow the trail. They pass a wooden signpost, on which is carved, TO THE MANTICORE, and before long they arrive at a large cage, where the promise of the sign is fulfilled.

The manticore's body is very like the body of a black panther, but it has a head like a middle-aged man's, with a receding hairline and a dark beard as coarse as thatch. The creature murmurs to itself as it paces restlessly to and fro, turning so

I
G
Z
U
H
K
R
G
Y

sharply when it reaches the limits of the cage that for a moment its forequarters and hindquarters travel in opposite directions.

'I regret to report that the distress caused by loneliness, insofar as which is meant a state of isolation from others of my kind, leaving me without recourse to either kith or kin, shows no sign of abatement,' states the manticore. 'I respectfully submit that, as circumstances present me with no hint of improvement, termination is now preferable to continuation, and I humbly beg to be provided with the means to end my existence.'

'What is this place?' says Crispin.

To her utter astonishment, Dessica finds that she knows the answer.

'Callisto talked to me about it this afternoon!' she gasps. 'He reckoned that some rich toff has been collecting demons. This must be the place.' Her intuition flashes again. 'That's what Aril's doing here!' she exclaims. 'The toff wants to add her to the collection.'

'Well I'm not going to let him!' Crispin says solemnly. 'Come on!'

The trail takes them away from the manticore's cage, around a corner, and there is Steyne House, standing on its rise, its windows golden-green with gaslight.

'She's in there,' says Crispin.

He attempts to walk on, but Dessica grabs him by the arm to prevent him.

'Time to make a proper plan, Crispin,' she opines.

Aril stands meekly in the middle of the Blue Drawing Room, and allows Kitty Montez to tend to the wound in the pad of her left forepaw. Kitty washes, salves and bandages the gash with a gentle tenderness.

'Not long now,' she says under her breath. 'Your friends are on their way.'

Aril's mind is hazy. She feels that she

ought to be someone else – that she *used* to be someone else – but just who that someone is eludes her. Her former life seems like a badly remembered dream, or a magic-lantern slide projected onto a billowing cloud of smoke.

Erasmus Slike, whose nerves are wound tighter than a watch spring, keeps close to the door. From the moment he first met Kitty, he was aware that she was unlike other women; now he is forced to wonder if she is not too unlike for his liking. No other female of his acquaintance would be quite so phlegmatic about nursing a werewolf.

Lord Bortle has felt ever so much more secure since he provided himself with a revolver from a hidden compartment in a nearby writing desk, and he keeps the weapon as close as a toddler keeps a comfort-blanket. He is, however, far from content, and he glances disapprovingly at Aril.

'One isn't convinced by this,' he says sulkily. 'On the whole, one would rather have one's dragon back.'

'That is unfortunate, my lord, but give it no mind,' advises Kitty. 'All will soon be taken away.'

'What, by death, d'you mean?' says Lord Bortle. 'One has that in hand. A swami is looking into it for one. The result will no doubt be pricey, but what's the use of money if one can't purchase immortality with it?'

A piercing whistle causes the earl to start, and then he starts once more as a boy cartwheels into the room through the open French windows, springs upright, and spreads his grin and his arms wide.

'Who the blazes are you?' demands Lord Bortle, rising from his chair. 'Where have you come from?'

'London, guv!' Crispin chirrups. 'I'm a cheery London sparrow who's come to tickle your funny bone.'

Lord Bortle is about to raise the pistol, but is distracted when Crispin, who has been taking lessons from Callisto, apparently produces an egg from his left ear. Crispin cracks the egg, which contains a posy of paper violets; he claps, and the flowers vanish.

Lord Bortle's laughter is like the barking of a seal.

'By Jupiter, that's terribly good, boy!' he says. 'What did you say your name was?'

He never receives a reply, for at that moment, Dessica Flaunt creeps up behind him and thwacks the back of his skull with a truncheon. The pistol tumbles to the carpet, closely followed by Lord Bortle, whose senseless body drops like a sack of potatoes.

Kitty holds up the Siren Stone.

'Come one step closer, and I shall command Aril to attack you!' she threatens. 'How delicious! I do believe this is an impasse.'

Dessica stoops to retrieve Lord Bortle's firearm, which she handles with manifest expertise.

'And I believe this is called a Colt Peacemaker,' she says.

'Don't be ridiculous, child!' snorts Kitty. 'It's quite obvious that you don't have the heart to kill me.'

'True,' agrees Dessica. 'But I wouldn't mind hurting you a bit. I could shoot off one of your thumbs, say, or the end of your nose.' She releases the gun's safety-catch, and cocks the hammer.

Erasmus Slike clears his throat, and addresses Dessica as if she were a Parliamentary session.

'Far be it from me to interfere in what is a somewhat delicate situation,' he begins, 'but at this juncture I feel compelled to recommend that no one commit any act of hastiness which may be regretted at some future, and less fraught juncture.'

'Shut your gob, matey!' commands Dessica. 'No one asked you nothing.' She lifts up the pistol and sights along the barrel. 'Fancy a new parting, missus?' she says.

Chapter Nineteen:
A Bargain with a Demon

Aboard the traction engine Dotty, Callisto keeps a watchful eye on the revolving gazetteer. Beneath a protective glass panel, rollers wind down a map of the terrain immediately west of Wolveston, at a rate commensurate with Dotty's speed. An articulated red needle indicates her approximate position.

To Callisto, progress seems deadly slow.

'Next turning to the left!' he calls out.

'Right you are,' affirms Hercules Popplewell. He turns the two wheels that control the attitude of Dotty's tracks, and the engine sweeps into a majestic curve.

'I'm not that keen on travelling this far west of a night-time,' Hercules confesses.

VKMGYAY

'I like streetlights, me. Hereabouts is a bit too murky for my taste.'

'There are worse murks than the night,' asserts Callisto.

At last the gates of Steyne House are in view. Callisto notes the gatekeeper in his kiosk, and his mind works rapidly. He calculates how much time it would take to stop the traction engine, request and be denied entry, and then apply money or mesmerism in order to change the gatekeeper's mind. The result is too much time.

'Hercules,' says Callisto, 'could Dotty knock down those gates?'

Hercules titters.

'Let's give it a go and see, shall we?' he says. 'Full steam, Charlie!'

'Aye,' says Charlie Chiddock, and re-doubles his shovelling efforts.

The gatekeeper sees the engine bearing down, and runs for his life as he realizes it is not going to stop.

With a dreadful grinding clang, Dotty runs full tilt into the ornamental ironwork. The shock of the impact jolts the hinges from their moorings in the stone arch, and the gates topple with a great crash. Dotty trundles over them as demurely as a maiden aunt picking her way down a muddy lane.

Callisto looks along the driveway to Steyne House, and whispers a mantra that sharpens his senses. Before long, he picks out the open windows on the ground floor, and shortly afterwards he discerns Aril, Kitty Montez, Dessica Flaunt and Crispin Rattle. Dessica, he observes, is holding a gun.

There is no time for Callisto to guess how Dessica and Crispin come to be at Steyne House. As Dotty enters the main courtyard and Hercules applies the brakes, Callisto jumps down from the cab, sprints to the terrace, and enters the Blue Drawing Room via the French windows.

V
K
M
G
Y
A
Y

'At last!' Kitty crows triumphantly.

Callisto dispenses with the routine niceties of salutation, raises his right arm and motions with his fingers. A ball of pale-blue fire erupts from his palm and bursts over Kitty, drenching her with flames. Her hair and dress ignite; her face sags as its flesh melts and drips like candle wax.

'Kitty, my angel!' sobs Erasmus Slike.

But he is weeping over someone who never was.

As the outer sham of Kitty Montez burns away, the true form of the demon Bazimaal swells up out of her smoking remains. The unharmed Siren Stone still glows and pulses in the demon's grasp.

Bazimaal is close to seven feet tall. It has the head and torso of a man, with skin the colour of cream of tomato soup. Its nose is hooked, its mouth is cruel, and its chin is tufted with a beard like a goat's. Ram's horns sprout from its temples, and from the waist down it has the hind-quarters of a bull.

This radical alteration in the appearance of his inamorata proves too much for Erasmus, and he crumples into a faint.

Callisto lifts his left hand, and a blur of magic shimmers in the air around it.

'Don't!' bellows Bazimaal.

'Give me a reason not to,' Callisto says darkly.

'Your ward's will is trapped inside this Siren Stone, and if you kill me, she will live out the rest of her days as a puppet with severed strings,' asserts Bazimaal. 'Let's parley!'

'Watch it, Mr Callisto, it might be a trick!' Crispin warns.

Bazimaal sniggers.

'Naturally it is a trick, boy,' it sneers. 'A demon can't help playing tricks and creating illusions, any more than your mentor Callisto can. Tricks are our stock in trade.'

'But my tricks aren't intended to overthrow governments,' says Callisto.

Bazimaal lashes its tail, and smashes a priceless antique vase on a nearby occasional table.

'Governments?' it repeats derisively. 'Do you honestly think that I take any interest at all in the way that humans manage their political affairs? I used the League of the Golden Unicorn as I used the Siren Stone – as a means to an end.'

'What end?' puzzles Callisto.

'Why, to bring you here, to the Fabulary Garden,' Bazimaal reveals. It points a black talon at the prostrate Lord Bortle. 'That degenerate vermin caused innocent creatures to be plucked from their rightful worlds and incarcerated here, where they do not belong. Their psychic howls of despair have resounded throughout all Inferno for months. The inhabitants of Inferno find the suffering of humans rich and satisfying, but the suffering of these demon beasts is insupportable, and must be made to cease.'

'Then slaughter them,' suggests Callisto.

'No!' cries Dessica, who still has the pistol trained on Bazimaal, though now she is supporting its weight with both hands. 'That ain't right, Callisto. They don't deserve to die. They ain't done nothing.'

'Well said, child,' Bazimaal murmurs. 'Why don't you put that gun down, for it's no protection against me. A bullet would do me about as much damage as a portion of mushy peas would do to a battleship.' It turns back to Callisto. 'The creation of the Fabulary Garden upset the fine balance between the worlds. To restore it, the creatures must be sent back.'

'Then do so,' Callisto says with a shrug.

Bazimaal purses its lips, waggles its fingers, shuffles its hooves, and manifests every sign of being embarrassed – if a demon is capable of such a feeling.

V
K
M
G
Y
A
Y

V
K
M
G
Y
A
Y

'Ah, but that would be to do a kindness and I, as you well know, am devious and malign. It is simply not in my power to perform an act whose outcome could, in any way, be considered good,' it admits. 'You, on the other hand, are in possession of a Portal Mirror.'

Callisto sees all in a trice.

'You wish to strike a bargain,' he proposes. 'If I return the demon animals to their home worlds, you will return Aril's willpower.'

'Exactly,' says Bazimaal.

Callisto frowns. 'Why didn't you come to me and ask for my help in the first place? Was there really a need for all this rigmarole?'

Bazimaal laughs cynically.

'And if I had turned up at Scarlatti Mews and spun my yarn, you would have believed me, would you?' it enquires. 'You would have set aside your hatred of me in order to restore cosmic harmony?

I think not! And besides, leading the League of the Golden Unicorn up the garden path amused me. Now, are you agreeable to my bargain?'

'I cannot trust you to keep your side of it,' Callisto says.

'Of course you can't!' says Bazimaal, in an aggrieved tone. 'What kind of demon do you take me for?'

'Then I require you to restore my ward at once!' insists Callisto.

Bazimaal whispers to the Siren Stone. 'You are released!'

Aril trembles. The werewolf sinks back inside her, and her usual self emerges. She sways.

Crispin flies to her side and braces her by placing an arm around her shoulders. He leads her to a sofa, on which she sits, rubbing her forehead and assuring him that she is quite all right.

'I must be leaving soon,' Bazimaal says to Callisto. 'But before I do, I must find a

gift to appease Dargaz the Tongue-Stretcher.' It indicates Lord Bortle. 'Are you sentimentally attached to him in any way?'

'None,' replies Callisto.

'What would be the reaction were he to disappear entirely?' Bazimaal muses.

'Indifference,' adjudges Callisto.

Bazimaal mocks its enemy with a bow. 'Until we meet again, Callisto.'

'When we meet again, I shall kill you,' Callisto swears.

'You may try,' says Bazimaal.

The world seems to give a little wink, and Bazimaal, Lord Bortle and the Siren Stone are gone from it.

Callisto declines all offers of assistance, maintaining that he is best left to himself. Aril, Crispin and Dessica go in search of Mrs Moncrief, while Callisto binds together Erasmus Slike's wrists before reviving him, and entrusting him to the care of Hercules Popplewell and Charlie Chiddock, who agree to turn him over to the Custodiate as soon as they return to Wolveston.

Then Callisto takes the copper Portal Mirror from the doctor's bag he has carried with him all night, steps out into the Fabulary Garden, and commences to put right the wrongs that were instigated by Lord Bortle.

M
U
X
M
U
T

Chapter Twenty:
The Wrath of the People

At daybreak, four hundred cavalrymen who have sworn loyalty to Mariah Stuart ride their mounts through a yellowish mist, and enter the easternmost end of Gospelmaker Road, the Scarp's most vital and most strategic artery. The men wear short Prussian-blue jackets with gold frogging, and bell-top shakos which bear white ostrich-feather plumes. They are equipped with carbines, revolvers and sabres, and bring no artillery with them since their commander, Field Marshal Sir Jarvis Barkshaw, has decided upon a short, sharp and flexible attack, intended to spread the maximum panic among the populace. The troops are arranged in eight evenly spaced blocks. Sir Jarvis and Brigadier Plumpton Drury ride in the front rank of the leading block.

The field marshal is in a confident mood. He expects the support of the Navy, the Press, the Church and the Banks, but in this he is self-deluded. Thanks to the discreet efficiency of the Custodiate, the League of the Golden Unicorn's would-be naval mutineers are already in irons, its archbishop has resigned and gone into exile on the Continent, its bankers have had their assets frozen and the newspaper editors are behind bars. However, Sir Jarvis remains a man to be reckoned with, supported or not. Four hundred armed soldiers can, by themselves, wreak considerable havoc upon a city of unprepared civilians.

'The scent of victory is in the air, Plummy!' the field marshal remarks. 'Funny thing, but it smells of chicory essence.'

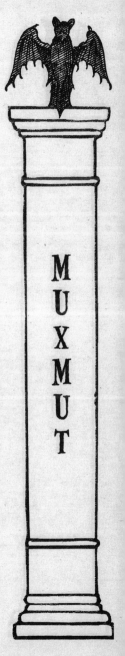

MUXMUT

The brigadier, who can smell nothing beyond the stench of a neighbouring tannery, nods, and changes the subject.

'Don't you find it peculiar that we had no more cables after midnight, sir?' he says. 'I would have thought that Operation Osiris would require a certain degree of co-ordination.'

'Covert campaign, Plummy!' barks Sir Jarvis. 'Telegraphic silence. Counting on those who count on you. No leaks, catch the enemy unawares.'

'Oh, absolutely, sir!' the brigadier enthuses; then his manner changes, and he frowns. 'All the same, sir, I can't help doubting if the enemy actually is unaware. Have you noticed how all the doors and windows have been boarded up?'

The field marshal glances to left and right, and sees that this is so.

'Consider the environs, Plummy!' he snorts. 'Scarp's swarming with degenerates. Can't keep their fingers out of other people's pockets. Rob their unborn grand-children if they could. Uncivilized, Plummy. Not human – not in the way you and I are. Their deaths, a merciful release.' He starts and stares. 'What's that up ahead?'

He points to a shadowy shape that runs across the road.

Brigadier Drury orders a halt, takes out his field-glasses and applies them to his face, just as a breath of breeze blows aside a wreath of mist. He sees a bulwark of detritus, a raggle-taggle heap of up-turned carts, cabs, barrows, kitchen tables, wardrobes and grandfather clocks.

'Vaulting Vortigern, it's a barricade, sir!' he gawps.

'Eyes must be playing tricks on you, Plummy,' derides the field marshal. 'People round here aren't organized enough to build a barricade.'

Brigadier Drury alters the focus of his binoculars.

MUXMUT

'Yes they are, sir,' he counters. 'And what's more, they have weapons!'

As if in illustration, a shot rings out, and a whistling bullet cleanly clips the plume off the field marshal's shako.

On the top of the barricade, wearing a white blouse that leaves her shoulders bare, and a flared crimson skirt, Squalida MacHeath thrusts a smoking six-gun into the belt at her waist. She unfurls the battle flag of the Protectorate – a broken yellow crown on a black background – and shouts, 'Let's go get 'em!'

With a tumultuous cheer, people spill over the barricade in a wild charge.

Sir Jarvis's face whitens, for he is confronted with a force more deadly than any dragon, and more formidable than the deepest secret conspiracy: the united wrath of the people. His heart and courage skip a beat.

'Fall back!' he bawls. 'Fall back!'

The retreating cavalrymen run into the

ranks of their comrades in the rear, and a debacle ensues.

Some hours later, in the officers' mess at Toolham Barracks, a battered and haggard Field Marshal Barkshaw downs a triple brandy in a single gulp, belches, and says, 'Ghastly, Plummy! Can't understand what went wrong.'

Brigadier Drury, who is seated on the opposite side of the table from the field marshal, looks equally battered. One of his epaulettes is missing, and his right eye is bruised and swollen.

'I can, sir,' he says. 'We underestimated our enemy. They demonstrated more fighting spirit than we thought them capable of. In the end, they were simply too good for us.'

The field marshal shakes his head.

'No, no, Plummy, can't be doing with that!' he rasps. 'Retreat and regroup, that's the ticket. Roll back and mop up.'

M
U
X
M
U
T

251

MUXMUT

A signals sergeant carrying a sheet of paper enters the mess. He crosses to the field marshal, clicks his heels together, salutes, and hands Sir Jarvis the paper.

'The break in the telegraph wire has been repaired, sir!' he announces. 'Captain Pinsen thinks it was cut by Custodiate agents, sir!'

The sergeant salutes again, and departs.

'The Custodiate, eh?' grunts the field marshal. 'It's all up if they're onto us.'

He peruses the paper. It is a cable from Paris, and it reads:

```
DEAR ALL - STOP - THANK YOU SO
MUCH FOR YOUR RECENT KIND OFFER
- STOP - I REGRET THAT I MUST
DECLINE IT AS YESTERDAY I ACCEPTED
A PROPOSAL OF MARRIAGE AND MY FIANCÉ
IS A STAUNCH REPUBLICAN - STOP -
SINCEREST GOOD WISHES MARIAH STUART
```

Sir Jarvis flings the paper onto the table. 'Had it, Plummy!' he sighs. 'Suppose I shall be exiled to some remote coral atoll in the Pacific.'

'Yes, sir,' agrees the brigadier, 'I suppose that you shall.'

By the time the Fabulary Garden is empty, the morning is well advanced and the sun is bright. Wearily, Callisto makes his way to the demolished gates of Steyne House, where he finds Aril, Crispin and Dessica asleep in the cab, whose driver's seat holds Mrs Moncrief, dozing snugly beneath a cabbie's blanket. Callisto gently wakes her from her slumbers, and the cab sets off eastwards, towards Wolveston and the risen sun.

'What's to be done now, Mr Callisto?' says Mrs Moncrief.

'Now we must go home and sit out the storm,' Callisto responds. 'There will be a great scandal – the greatest since the monarchy was abolished. Investigations will be conducted, and trials held. We can

M
U
X
M
U
T

expect resignations, revelations and repercussions for months to come, perhaps years. The nation's faith in itself will be sorely tried.'

'I meant, what's to be done with Miss Flaunt?' Mrs Moncrief corrects her employer.

Callisto contrives to be both defensive and wheedling. 'Since you are the utter paragon of housekeepers, Mrs M, and since it would be the easiest thing in the world to have the attic converted into a bedroom, I wonder if you would have any objections to Dessica's becoming a permanent addition to the household?'

'Just a minute, matey!' snaps a muffled voice.

The flap of the communication hatch flicks back, and a portion of Dessica's face appears in the hatchway.

'I heard that!' she says. 'Live with you lot? You must think I'm cracked or something. Keep your demons, and traitors, and pistol-packing toffs to yourselves, I'd rather deal with floaters any day. Squalida MacHeath paid me a tidy sum for that there notebook, and I'm going to buy myself a comfy crib with it. I've managed without anybody's charity so far, and that's how it's going to stay. There's just one thing I want from you, Callisto.'

'What?'

'That League of the Golden Unicorn,' says Dessica. 'What have unicorns got to do with it?'

'A unicorn appears on the coat of arms of the Stuart family,' Callisto explains.

'Much obliged!' says Dessica. She closes the hatch, settles back in her seat, and notices that Crispin is awake, and staring at her. 'What?' she demands.

'You might not be coming to live in Scarlatti Mews, but we'll still be friends, won't we?' says Crispin. 'You'll pop in for a chat every now and then, won't you?'

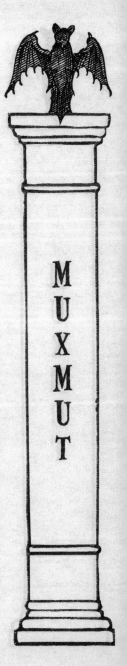

'I'll think about it,' says Dessica.

'Does that mean yes or no?'

'I'm a river girl,' Dessica says enigmatically. 'You never can tell with river girls.'

Epilogue

Inferno's most populous city is Torquedorum, a place of the most ingenious diablerie. One of Torquedorum's broadest boulevards starts in a square surrounded by outlandish buildings, whose Cyclopean masonry towers into the blood-red sky at vertiginous and impossible angles. The traffic that passes through the square is indescribable; the crowds that frequent it are unspeakable.

At the centre of the square stands a plinth which supports a cage, and huddled in the cage is the naked and quaking form of Lord Bortle. The earl's eyes are bloodshot and unblinking; his hair has turned completely white. He lives a life of public squalor, and has no privacy.

MUXMUT

Morning, noon and night have no meaning in Inferno. Time is a relentless red glare. Passers-by continually mock, mortify and mistreat the prisoner in the cage. He is reviled, and spat upon, and subjected to humiliations beyond imagining.

Nevertheless, the lord still retains an iota of personal identity, for every now and then he pleads, 'Might one be allowed a butler? A maidservant? A cook? A stable boy?'

These protestations occasion much hilarity among his tormentors, who venture wagers on when the next outburst will be. Otherwise Lord Bortle's words are merely gibberish, and their sound is lost amidst the hurly-burly of the throng, and the distant roaring of eternal fires.

FABULOUS CREATURES!

Lord Bortle's Fabulary Garden is full of amazing creatures, but his menagerie is not complete. Throughout the book there is one pillar for each chapter with the name of a fabulous creature inscribed upon it. Decode the names to discover the creatures. But take care! The images at the tops of the pillars show mostly the more mundane types of creature – dogs, bats and big cats, for instance – to fool the casual visitor into believing that Lord Bortle's collection is simply a rich man's folly, rather than a place of evil with creatures captured solely for his own pleasure. Only by decoding the names can you discover the amazing beasts which Lord Bortle likes to display – including both those he already has in his collection, and those which he would like to get his nasty hands on . . .

CAESAR'S CODE

To crack this code, use the magic number 7. A is the first letter of the alphabet and that becomes G, the seventh letter of the alphabet. B then becomes H, C becomes I and so on. Use the grid below to decode the creatures.

A = U	**B** = V	**C** = W	**D** = X
E = Y	**F** = Z	**G** = A	**H** = B
I = C	**J** = D	**K** = E	**L** = F
M = G	**N** = H	**O** = I	**P** = J
Q = K	**R** = L	**S** = M	**T** = N
U = O	**V** = P	**W** = Q	**X** = R
Y = S	**Z** = T		

A Glossary of the Weird and Wonderful Beasties and Creatures you should find

AFANC
A monster resembling a giant beaver, the Afanc is rumoured to be found in the lakes, pools and rivers of North Wales.

BASILISK
A four-legged cockerel with the tail of a snake. Its breath and look are fatal.

CATOBELAS
A black buffalo with a boar's head. This unfortunate creature's head is so heavy, it is not strong enough to lift it, so it hangs close to the ground.

CENTAUR
A man to the waist. Below the waist, the body, legs and tail of a horse. Centaurs are as clever as humans. Wine drives them into a frenzy.

CHIMERA
A beast with a lion's head and front paws, the body of a goat and a serpent's tail.

DRAGON
A gigantic, fire-breathing, winged serpent. The Chinese dragon has a more snakelike body than its European cousin, and a less aggressive and destructive nature.

GORGON
A woman with live snakes on her head instead of hair, and brass claws. A single glance from a gorgon turns people into stone.

GRYPHON (OR GRIFFIN)
A monster with the head and wings of an eagle, and a lion's body.

HARPIES
Winged creatures resembling women-headed vultures. They tear their hapless victims into shreds.

KRAKEN
A vast, squid-like creature which dwells in the gloomiest depths of the ocean.

MANTICORE
The manticore has a man's head and a lion's body.

MERMAID
Mermaids are fair maidens who have the tails of fish instead of legs. Friendly in nature, they often sing to sailors, and sometimes rescue them from drowning.

PEGASUS
A mighty winged horse, Pegasus was ridden by the Ancient Greek hero Bellerophon.

SALAMANDER
A poisonous lizard which is capable of surviving in the heart of a fierce fire.

SATYR
A small horned creature with a human torso and the hind-quarters of a goat, satyrs are fond of music, and dancing with nymphs.

SELKIE

Selkies are Scottish beasts. They are humans who are able to take the form of seals.

TROLL

Approximately human in appearance, trolls are giant goblins. Some have two or three heads. Trolls are notoriously slow-witted.

UNICORN

A pure white horse with a single horn growing out of its forehead. Unicorns are fond of eating liquorice roots, which make their breath smell sweet.

WEREWOLF

Werewolves are humans who become wolves, or appear wolf-like, when the moon is full.

WYVERN (OR WIVERN)

A winged dragon with the tail of a snake.

SOURCES

J. L. Borges: *The Book of Imaginary Beings*
Brewer's Dictionary of Phrase and Fable
K. Briggs: *A Dictionary of Fairies*
R. Greene: *Pandosto*

ABOUT THE AUTHOR

Matt Hart is Welsh and proud of it – so mind now. As a child he caught measles, chickenpox, whooping cough and German measles (five times). He has worked on a fairground (as the innards of an 'automatic' prize-dispensing machine), in an architect's office, as a bus conductor, and as a general labourer on a building site.

Matt reads loads and isn't much of a dab hand at anything. He always looks untidy, even when he's wearing expensive clothes. His favourite animal is the coati-mundi.

Matt is married and lives in Berkshire.

THE BLACK SPHINX

The **BLACK SPHINX**
is missing. *Who wants it the most?*

THE INDOMITABLE
CALLISTO?

Queen OF THE *Underworld*
SQUALIDA MacHEATH?

OR · MADDER · THAN · A · MACKEREL
JASPER PEPPER?

Or will it be
CRISPIN RATTLE,

OUR **ORPHANED** YOUNG HERO?
But if **JACKAL-HEADED GODS** can't stop
JASPER PEPPER,

what on earth can **CRISPIN** do?

CAN YOU CRACK THE HIEROGLYPHIC CODE?

'Rip-roaring tale . . . a real "hiss-the-villain" adventure'
JUNIOR NEWS & MAIL

ISBN 978 0 552 55421 3